Cousins In Action

Operation Tiger Paw

Cousins In Action

Operation Tiger Paw

* * *

Sam Bond

Cover Art by

Han Randhawa

BOUND PUBLISHING / AUSTIN, TX

Sam Bond/Bound Publishing
P O Box 161081
Austin, TX, 78716
www.5cousinsadventures.com

Publisher's Note: This is a work of fiction. Names, characters, places, and incidents are a product of the author's imagination. Locales and public names are sometimes used for atmospheric purposes. Any resemblance to actual people, living or dead, or to businesses, companies, events, institutions, or locales is completely coincidental.

Illustrations copyright 2014 Han Randhawa
All rights reserved

Book design © 2014, BookDesignTemplates.com

First Edition vs 1.

ISBN 978-0-9911914-3-7

[1. India – Fiction. 2. Tigers – Fiction. 3. Cousins – Fiction. 4. Adoption – Fiction. 5. Travel – Fiction. 6. Spy – Fiction. 7. Adventure – Fiction 8. Mystery – Fiction]

Printed in the United States of America

For my girls, Olivia and Tess

"I knew when I met you an adventure was going to happen." – Winnie The Pooh

adventure [ad-ven-ture]
1. an undertaking, usually involving danger and risk.

2. an exciting or remarkable experience.

3. an adventure involving financial risk.

1

The Locked Study

Olivia and Tess' parents flew to France, so they sent the girls to Lissy's. Lissy's parents traveled to Turkey. So they sent the girls to Cagney and Aidan's. Cagney and Aidan's parents ended up in Egypt. And that's how five cousins, Olivia, Tess, Lissy, Cagney and Aidan, all found themselves at Grandma's house, for what they imagined would be a very dull time indeed. How wrong could five cousins be?

It was one of those hot summer days so typical in Texas. A day where the entire population snoozes under the rays of an unforgiving sun. Or, failing that, is inside enjoying man's greatest invention – air conditioning. Unfortunately for the cousins, they were neither snoozing, nor inside. Instead, they lay spread beneath a large live oak in various degrees of boredom.

Aidan lay sprawled against the tree trunk reading his library book, *Leprechauns: An Owner's Manual*, and had just got to a really good bit about the dietary needs of the fully grown male. His eyes widened. Aidan never knew anyone could eat so much cabbage, well, not without having their nose pinched. He wrinkled his brow at the thought and gave thanks Leprechanism did not run in the family – at least, he was pretty sure it didn't.

Inserting a book-mark between chapters, he wondered about the author, Peevish McNoodle's, choice of page color, a shade best described as being halfway between peas and puke. Well, it was definitely different. And different was good, right?

Aidan eyed his youngest cousin, Tess, coasting to and fro on the tree swing. Now *there* was someone distinctly different. Aidan smiled as her pink lace tutu fluttered in the non-existent breeze.

And then there was his sister, Cagney. Squatting beside a bedraggled toadstool, her brand new Canon in one hand, batting a befuddled butterfly with the other, Cagney would hate to be thought of as different. As the oldest, she wanted nothing more than to fit in. Unfortunately, and as she was not afraid to remind people, she'd been lumbered with a family of misfits, thank you very much, and, all things considered, it really wasn't her fault.

Aidan's eyes swept past Cagney and focused on the feet sticking out the end of the swinging hammock. The toes, the frill of a yellow sundress and a laptop with the words 'Spider' engraved across it was all he could actually see of his cousin, Lissy, but it was enough. Lissy was an only child and Spider went everywhere with her. Spider was her companion and friend; a friend with whom she was currently having a heated discussion.

His eyes moved to Olivia, who was practicing walking backwards … on her hands. Yep, there was no getting away from it, his family was definitely different. Decidedly so.

Cagney slumped onto the porch. She was sweaty. She was cranky, and she wasn't afraid to show it. "Has anyone had any luck breaking into Grandma's study today?"

"Nope," said the others together.

Tess kicked back the swing and arched through the air. "My pink fluffy tutu can't believe she put another lock on it."

Cagney scowled. "Has anyone tried a paperclip?"

"Twice," said Olivia.

Lissy shook her head. "I can't believe she doesn't trust us."

"I know, her own flesh and blood. Honestly, it's appalling the lack of trust this family has," said Cagney.

Olivia flipped onto her feet and stretched like a cat. "I almost got in yesterday, but Mrs. Snoops knocked at the door. I barely escaped before Grandma's slippers came shuffling down the hallway."

Mrs. Snoops was a kindly neighbor, whose incredibly large underwear always seemed to be hanging out to dry.

"After Peru, you'd think Grandma would cut us some slack," said Aidan.

"She abandons us in the middle of South America," said Lissy, "then pretends like nothing happened."

"I thought she'd be proud of us," said Tess.

"She's definitely bleating around the bush," said Cagney, with one of her typical misquotes.

It was one week since the cousins arrived back from Peru. They had returned home, showered, changed, and then, in Cagney's case, showered some more. Then they waited for the inevitable: the phone calls from work and their parents explaining, yet again, how they were needed on various sides of the globe.

At first they were pleased to be together. Even Cagney couldn't hide the excitement of reliving their adventure in Peru, but that was where it ended. Somehow, Grandma managed to completely avoid answering any and all questions about what she'd done, where she'd been, and what had become of the treasure they'd discovered while in South America. It was, as Lissy pointed out, "extremely disappointing."

Olivia approached the live oak, and using Aidan's head as a stepping stone, started to clamber skyward. Half-way up, she shimmied along a branch and, regaining her balance, eyed the five-foot gap between where she stood and where she wanted to stand.

Cagney brushed the frizz of hair from her forehead and squinted towards the tree. "You think that's going to work? You've got to admit, it wasn't exactly the best idea you've had."

Lissy rolled her eyes. If her memory served correctly, and it always did, it was Cagney's idea to climb onto the roof to see into Grandma's study. Mind you, it wasn't like Olivia didn't have her own hair-brained ideas. In fact, in the scheme of things, this one was pretty mellow. Most of them landed Olivia in a bucket load of trouble. Lissy was under no illusion this one would end any differently.

She also knew Olivia wouldn't care. Getting in trouble never bothered Olivia. In fact, Lissy was beginning to think she enjoyed it. In nine years she could only remember seeing Olivia cry once, when her dog, Roofus, got hit by a car. Lissy was sure

Olivia loved animals more than people. Lissy was right.

"You'll never make it," yelled Cagney, shoving her replacement glasses back up the bridge of her nose.

"I thought you didn't approve of Olivia climbing on the roof," said Lissy.

"Who me?" said Cagney, trying to look innocent and failing.

"You said she'd break a leg," said Tess, dragging the swing to a stop.

Cagney scowled. "That was before."

"Before what?" asked Tess.

Aidan ducked behind the lime green Leprechaun book. "Before she became so darn nosey."

Cagney gave her brother one of her looks. Cagney was known for giving looks. Lissy swore she once saw Cagney wilt a cactus with one. Luckily, her younger brother, Aidan, was too good natured to take them personally.

"If only we'd gone into the study when Grandma invited us," said Lissy.

Grandma's study and, in particular, her closet was something of a mystery. A mystery the five were longing to solve. Each cousin had been told a tale by grandma guaranteed to keep them as far away from the study as possible. Which, of course, had the exact opposite effect. Honestly, grown-ups could be so dumb.

The cousins had deduced there was something Grandma didn't want them to see. But that was as far as they'd got.

"I told her I wanted to see her Barbie collection," said Tess. "But she told me Hiss had eaten them."

"I told her I wasn't scared of ghosts anymore," said Lissy. "But she said they'd gone on vacation."

Aidan scratched his head. "When I think of all the times she asked us to come see–"

"The ghosts," interrupted Lissy.

"The rats," said Cagney.

"If only we'd known," said Aidan.

Tess stuffed a plum into her mouth and did her best to form words. "Known what?" she spluttered.

"Known she had a secret," said Cagney, watching with disgust, as plum juice trickled its way down Tess' chin.

Lissy looked up as Olivia launched herself from the live oak, landing with a thud on the roof. Regaining her balance, Olivia scrambled towards the edge. Pausing above the window she reached into the back of her shorts and pulled out a pair of gloves. Crouching, she shoved them onto her fingers before gripping the gutters. Once she had a firm hold, she leaned far over the edge.

From the ground, the cousins had found it impossible to see into Grandma's study. Dense blinds covered two windows and much to their annoyance, they were always closed. But at the top, Olivia had spied a tiny gap. A gap she now had her eye pressed against.

"Can you see anything?" asked Aidan.

"I'm not sure," said Olivia. "I think I might be able to see a ..."

"A what?" asked Cagney, scrambling to her feet.

"A ... a ... Stonehenge," said Olivia.

Grandma Callie was born in England and a variety of weird English objects littered her home. The cousins had been subjected to more tales of life in England from their fathers and Grandma than they cared to remember. All the cousins wanted to know was, if England was so great, why had their whole family moved here?

Grandma had not visited England in a long time. In fact, as far as the cousins were aware, Grandma had not visited *anywhere* until just over a week ago. For years she'd lived in a small Texas town with a cat named Chaos, a snake named Hiss and a cactus named Percy. But then the phone calls started and everything changed. Aidan couldn't help but wonder how long it would be until they started again?

"What else can you see, Olivia?" Tess rose and, balancing on the tips of her pink sparkly sandals, peered up at her precariously perched sister.

"You know, guys, it's kind of hard to see from this position," said Olivia, shuffling forward on her belly.

The phone in the study let out a trill.

Lissy gulped. "Olivia quick, get down."

"No, stay up," said Cagney.

Olivia glared at her cousins. "Could you put a cork in it?"

"Let the girl listen, will you?" said Aidan.

Cagney fell silent and studied Olivia with rapt attention.

"Grandma's in the room. She's picking up the phone. She's nodding. She's nodding some more. Now she's shaking – nope, she's nodding again."

"Oh for goodness sake," cried Cagney. "Could she make up her mind?"

"Now she's writing something. Yep, she's put down the phone and she's heading towards the closet."

"Oooh, the closet," gasped Tess, almost toppling off the swing with excitement.

Lissy wrenched her gaze away from Spider. "What's in it?"

"I'm not sure. She's opening the door. She's reaching inside and …"

An ominous noise from behind the backdoor made Olivia pause. Suddenly, the cat flap flew open and, with a screech of claws and a blur of gray, Chaos, the cat, catapulted out of the house, tore across the grass and leapt into the live oak.

Lissy scratched her head. "What's wrong with Chaos?"

Chaos did not stop to answer, but continued to climb higher and higher until she was lost amongst the branches.

"Chaos, come down!" cried Tess.

"What?" said Olivia.

"Come down!" said Lissy.

"I thought you wanted me to staaaay ..." Olivia let out a piercing scream as her fists, sweaty from the gloves, released their grip and she toppled head first off the roof.

At that exact moment, the porch door swung open and Olivia dropped head first into the hands of a large, square man. A man dressed all in black.

2

Sneezy

The man raised an eyebrow. "Yo!"

"Hey, it's Sneezy, the pet sitter," said Aidan.

"The what?" asked the man.

Tess sprang from the swing and headed towards the pet sitter. "You look after Hiss and Chaos when Grandma goes out of town, right?"

"Oh, yeah. I do that. That's exactly what I do. I'm a …. yeah, a pet sitter."

Olivia craned her neck and took in the features of the huge, solid man. The blood was starting to rush to her head. "Erm … thanks for catching me."

The pet sitter glanced at Olivia. It was as if he'd forgotten an eleven-year-old Chinese child dangled upside down in his arms. In a spin, worthy of a world-class baton twirler, he flipped Olivia the right way, and gently placed her on her feet. "No worries."

"Don't you want to know what I was doing?"

"It's probably best you don't tell me. I'm not very good with secrets."

"Me neither," said Tess. "They always seem to spill out."

This was an understatement. Tess routinely not only put her foot in her mouth, but her entire leg. She didn't mean to, but Tess was what grown-ups routinely called a character. Tess had asked her father which character, "Cinderella? Mulan? Alice in Wonderland?" Her father had drawn her to him, rustled her thick black hair and given her the bad news. "I was thinking more like Winnie the Pooh."

Cagney studied the large dark man. She noted the pet sitter's wool jacket, his cashmere sweater and his black sunglasses. Cagney thought he was pulling off New York chic very well. Unfortunately, this was June in Texas and New York chic didn't cut it. "Can we help you?" she asked.

"I've come to get Chaos," said the pet sitter. "But she took one look at me and bolted."

Lissy pointed to the top of the live oak. "She's up there."

"Way up there," added Olivia.

The pet sitter pushed his sunglasses onto the top of his head and sighed. "I don't think she likes me."

"Don't worry," said Tess. "She doesn't like anyone. Well, other than Olivia."

"So, are you going to get her?" asked Aidan.

The pet sitter pursed his lips. "Get her?"

"Yes." Aidan clambered to his feet. "She's not going to come down by herself, you know."

"You're going to have to climb," said Lissy.

"Climb?"

"Yep," said Olivia. "It's easy."

"If you're nine," said the pet sitter.

"Hey!" Olivia folded her arms across her Red Sox tee. "I'm eleven!"

The pet sitter raised his eyebrows. "No need to get defensive. I was small when I was a kid too."

"Really?" Tess studied the humongous man. "What did your mom feed you?"

Being told how tiny they were was something the cousins were used to. At twelve, Cagney was the oldest; Tess, aged six, the youngest. Aidan, the only boy, was sandwiched in the middle. At school each was the smallest in their grade – by a lot.

Cagney adjusted her glasses and stared directly at the pet sitter. "You know, we saw you in Lima."

The pet sitter looked alarmed, his mouth opening and closing like a game of Hungry Hippos. Finally he cleared his throat. "Who? Me?"

"Aha!" said Tess.

"In Lima?" The pet sitter's eye began to twitch, a bead of sweat broke along his brow.

"In fact, we saw you several times," said Cagney.

"Really?" he swallowed hard. "That's unfortunate."

"Yep," said Olivia. "Do you have an explanation?"

"Do you need one?"

"It would be nice," said Lissy.

The pet sitter grunted. "Ya know, I'm kind of new at this. I think I should concentrate on getting Chaos."

And before the cousins could say any more, he set off towards the tree.

"Go Sneezy. My pink fluffy tutu knows you can do it," said Tess.

The pet sitter scowled. "Who are you calling Sneezy?"

Lissy lowered her head and glanced up shyly. "It's just a nickname."

"Remember last time you were here?" said Olivia. "You were all sneezy."

"I don't like nicknames," said the pet sitter, taking off his jacket and placing it on a wooden bench.

"Then what's your real name?" asked Cagney.

"A–gen …" the pet sitter faltered. "Now see what you made me do. I told you I wasn't good at keeping secrets."

"Your name's A-Jen?" asked Tess.

"No," the pet sitter replied. "It's Sneezy."

3

Chaos

Aidan swung his arms to the right. "To your left."

"Nope, to the right," said Tess.

"Down a bit," yelled Cagney.

"No, up," said Lissy.

Sneezy peered down at the cousins from the depths of the live oak and spat a large green leaf from between his lips. "I know you're all trying to be helpful," he said, as he slowly inched along a tree limb. "But you're not."

"Look, there she goes again!" Tess watched Chaos leap from branch to branch, further away from the pet sitter. Sneezy sighed loudly and climbed higher.

"You know, Olivia, you could get Chaos *for* him," suggested Aidan.

"Yeah, you're the only one she likes," said Cagney.

"In fact, she'd come if you called her," said Lissy.

"I know," said Olivia, with a wicked grin. "But what fun would that be?"

Tess wiped plum juice off her nose and flopped to the ground. "A-Jen is a really unusual name."

Lissy smiled and shook her head.

"Sneezy really *can't* keep a secret," said Olivia.

"It definitely makes you wonder, doesn't it?" said Cagney.

"Wonder what?" asked Tess.

"It would make a lot of sense," said Lissy.

"It opens doors to all sorts of possibilities," said Aidan.

"Possibilities?" said Tess. "What possibilities?"

"I can hardly believe it, though." Lissy closed Spider in favor of watching the rescue mission.

"Me neither," said Olivia, "but what other explanation is there?"

"Maybe his name really is A-Jen," said Aidan.

"Oh, his name," said Tess, finally understanding. "I know a lot of people with unusual names. Shu, Xiao, Liu–"

"They're not unusual." Olivia rolled her eyes. "They're Chinese."

"So, where do you think we're going this time?" asked Aidan.

"Going?" said Cagney. "Nobody said anything about going."

Aidan grinned at his sister. He wasn't a tease, but sometimes it was hard not to. On the other foot, Cagney was not above teasing Aidan. She teased him about his books. She teased him when girls from school talked to him. She even teased him when he got straight A's. Aidan didn't care. He knew his sister could be cranky. As far as he was concerned, that's what sisters were for.

Aidan lay back and watched Sneezy fight to keep his grip as he came face to tail with a fluffy squirrel. "Think about it. What happened last time Sneezy showed up?"

Olivia turned a cartwheel. "One day later, we were on a plane heading south."

"Oh no," gulped Lissy. "I'm barely over our last adventure. Grandma *can't* be going anywhere so soon?"

"You know Grandma," said Aidan.

"Actually we *don't* know Grandma. She's what they call 'mysterious'," said Olivia.

"I wonder where we'll go?" said Tess.

"I tell you, we're not going *anywhere*," said Cagney.

"I hope it's somewhere sandy," said Tess. "My pink sparkly sandals are itching to go somewhere sandy."

"Somewhere with exotic animals," said Olivia.

"Somewhere with internet connection," said Lissy.

"Hey, Sneezy!" yelled Tess. "Where's Grandma going this time?"

Olivia peered up, way up. Sneezy was shimmying along a very skinny branch. "Erm, I don't think you should do that."

"What?" said Sneezy.

"I said, it's best not to ..."

The tree produced a high-pitched crack and Olivia leapt backwards.

"Oh, that's not good," said Aidan. "Not good at all."

"Run!" yelled Cagney.

The branch tumbled through the tree, closely followed by Sneezy, flailing wildly.

The cousins scattered to the corners of the garden as Sneezy, and the tree limb, hit the ground.

"Ow!" came a muffled voice.

Lissy climbed through the wreckage and knelt by Sneezy's head. "Sir, are you okay?"

Sneezy was so covered in leaves, he resembled a curious mix between the Incredible Hulk and a giant cabbage. Lissy held out a hand and attempted to haul the pet sitter to a sitting position.

"Smile!" Cagney zoomed in and snapped a picture.

Sneezy scowled. "I'm fine." He spat out a twig. "It's all part of the service."

"Destroying a hundred-year-old live oak?" said Tess.

"It's not destroyed." Sneezy looked around. "It's, uh, trimmed."

"This is *not* a trim," said Cagney, grabbing a branch and waving it in Sneezy's face. "This is more your complete haircut."

"Oooh," said Tess, "Grandma's going to kill you!"

Sneezy climbed out of the leaves and brushed several twigs from his cashmere sweater. "Will not."

"Will too," said Cagney.

Suddenly the study window flew open and the silhouette of Grandma Callie was outlined against the glass. Aidan couldn't tell for sure, but he was pretty certain she wasn't happy.

4

The Journey

Cagney slumped into her seat, folded her arms and pouted. "I cannot believe we're going to India," she said, through gritted teeth.

Aidan reached forward and tapped his sister on her head with his battered copy of *Leprechauns: An Owner's Manual.* "I told you Grandma was going somewhere."

"And where Grandma goes, we go," said Olivia.

Olivia and Cagney swiveled around and hung over the back of their chairs to face their three cousins.

"It's going to be dreadful," said Cagney. "I hate Indian food. I'm going to starve!"

"I've always wanted to meet an Indian. How!" said Tess, raising her right hand.

"That's not right," said Cagney.

"Is too. I've seen the Lone Ranger. That's what they always say."

"But those aren't Indians," said Lissy.

"What do you mean they're not Indians?" asked Tess. "We're going to India, right?"

"Yep, but you're talking about Native American Indians. These are just … well, Indians," said Aidan.

"Hmm!" said Tess.

Olivia raised the blind and gazed out the small oval window at the clouds below. "Where *is* India?"

"It's in Asia." Lissy tapped at Spider. "It's the seventh largest country in the world and the second most populated after China."

"Hey, China wins," said Tess.

"I don't think it's a competition," said Aidan, kindly. "Sometimes it's really hard to feed everyone when you have so many people. A lot of people are very poor."

"Oh, that's sad," said Tess.

"Spider says China is one of the six countries bordering India," said Lissy. "India's surrounded by three different bodies of water and the world's tallest mountain range, the Himalayas, in the north."

Cagney rolled her eyes and slumped into her seat. "Fascinating! No really it's quite–"

Lissy shoved her feet in the back of Cagney's chair and pushed hard. Cagney always made fun of Spider. Lissy was used to it, but it didn't mean she liked it. Lissy enjoyed knowing facts, she was always happiest when she knew the answer. How boring life would be if you didn't have information and solutions.

Lissy grabbed Spider and gave her a hug. Sometimes she wished Spider was her cousin instead of Cagney. Spider only spoke the truth, didn't talk back and was never sarcastic. Yes, thought Lissy, Spider would make an excellent cousin.

Aidan ignored his sister's grumbling and gave Lissy an encouraging smile. "Aren't the Himalayas where Mount Everest is?"

Lissy cleared her throat and stopped shoving her feet in Cagney's back. "Yes. At 29,000 feet Mount Everest is the tallest mountain in the world. That's like me times." Lissy paused, "erm ... a lot."

Olivia yanked the blind back into position. "I wonder if we flew over Mount Everest when mom and dad brought us home from China?"

Olivia and Tess had been adopted from China when they were babies. It was so long ago no one could remember when they weren't all part of the same family. Sometimes people were surprised when they found out they were cousins, as having curly light hair, Cagney, Aidan and Lissy did not exactly look Chinese. However, to the five, they were all family. What they looked like didn't matter.

"You might have. Spider says India and China are about as far away from the U.S. as you can get. Doesn't matter whether you fly east or west. Either way it's going to take forever."

Cagney tapped her foot and glanced at her watch. "You don't say."

Cagney was about to say a whole lot more, but was interrupted by the flight attendant. She wore a long fitted skirt and a tight black top with a long piece of orange material flowing down off one shoulder. Her jet black hair was scraped off her face in a tightly wound bun and through her nose sat a tiny stud.

"May I get you anything to eat?" asked the flight attendant, indicating the food cart.

"Ooh, yes," said Tess. "Do you have any strawberries? Preferably with ice cream and accompanied by a banana?"

The flight attendant laughed, her heavy black eyelids creasing. "I'm afraid not. But I have curry."

"Then, I'd like beef curry, please," said Tess, tucking a large flowery napkin down the neck of her fuzzy pink tee.

"I am sorry, ma'am, but we do not eat beef in India. This is chicken curry."

"Why don't you eat beef?" asked Aidan.

"Because the cow is a sacred animal," replied the flight attendant.

"What about chickens?" asked Tess.

"Not so sacred," said the flight attendant, handing her a tray.

"Arrgh!" said Cagney. "This is going to be a nightmare."

"Don't worry, Miss. We also have cheese and macaroni."

"That'll do too." Tess took the foil-wrapped dish from the flight attendant's hands and tucked in.

Cagney frowned. "How on earth does she stay so thin?"

"It's a Chinese thing," said Olivia, who was just as slim as Tess, if not slimmer.

"Spider says there are people in India called *Jaines* who don't eat anything."

"What?" sputtered Tess.

"They believe everything has a soul, so they can't eat it," said Lissy.

"How do they survive?" asked Aidan, his mouth stuffed full of chicken.

"They only eat fruit that's fallen from trees," said Lissy. "Plus they rarely go out at night in case they step on something and squish it in the dark."

"That's just weird," said Olivia.

"Maybe they think eating animals is weird," said Aidan. "You never know."

"Aidan, are you going to learn Indian?" asked Tess.

In Peru, Aidan had learned Spanish so well he became almost fluent.

"India is so huge, it has over twenty official languages," said Lissy, tearing off some naan bread.

"Wow! How are you going to decide which one to learn?" asked Tess.

"Well, luckily the two main languages are Hindi and English. So at least we shouldn't have any problem being understood. But I do have this." Aidan held up a tattered-looking book bearing the words *Scribbling Sanskrit*. "I think I'll try and learn the written language."

"Why do Indians speak English?" asked Tess.

"Because the English colonized India when Queen Victoria sat on the throne," said Lissy.

"On the what?" asked Olivia.

"The throne," repeated Lissy.

Olivia scratched her head. "Yeah! That's what I thought you said."

Tess wiped curry off her forehead with the bottom of her pink fuzzy tee-shirt. "What does colonized mean?"

"It means people go to a new area and take over," said Aidan.

"A place where no one lives?" asked Tess.

"Nope, a place where people already live, but often those people are not considered as civilized," said Aidan. "Unfortunately, people take advantage."

Tess scratched her head. "People seem to have a habit of wanting other peoples' countries, don't they?"

Aidan yawned widely. "They sure do."

"Are you okay, Aidan?" asked Lissy.

"It's these tablets I took. They're supposed to be motion sickness pills, but they just make me sleepy."

"Does that mean you're not going to finish your chicken curry?" Leaning over, Tess forked a piece of yellow meat.

Aidan let out a snore.

Tess licked her lips and slid the entire tray onto the table in front of her. "I'll take that as a 'yes'."

"Excuse me?" said the flight attendant, gently shaking Tess.

"Hmm?" said Tess.

"We've landed."

Tess stretched her toes. "Landed where?"

"In New Delhi," said the flight attendant. "In fact, everyone else is already off."

"Off what?" asked Aidan, groggily.

"Off the plane," said the flight attendant.

"When you say everyone," said Olivia, rising. "You mean everyone except our grandma, right?"

The flight attendant shook her head. "No ma'am, I mean everyone."

5

Abandoned

Lissy was running to keep up with the flight attendant, who pounded through the airport at breakneck speed. For someone in a tight long skirt, she could really move.

"I cannot believe she's done it again," said Lissy, clutching Spider to her dress.

"Exciting, isn't it?" said Olivia.

"That's not *exactly* the word I was looking for," said Lissy.

Aidan grasped Tess' hand and dragged her along. "Come on slow poke. You don't want to get lost in New Delhi – we'd never find you."

"Who's going to look after us this time?" gasped Tess, trying to keep up.

"I'm not sure," said Aidan. "But I hope they're like Lucila. She was fun."

Lucila was the lady who showed the cousins around Lima. She was outgoing and colorful and probably the worst driver Aidan had ever met.

The flight attendant guided them through immigration and, after picking up their bags, ushered the cousins towards customs.

"Yikes!" said Cagney, stopping dead.

"Are you okay?" asked Lissy.

"I'd forgotten about customs," she replied.

"What about it? You fill in a form and go through," said Olivia, flapping the form dangerously close to Cagney's nose.

"What about the part asking if you have any food?"

"But we don't have any food," said Aidan.

"We have food?" asked Tess, perking up.

Cagney's cheeks glowed a delicate shade of scarlet. "We might have a little."

"Grandma only packed us cookies and that was over a day ago," said Olivia. "Chuck 'em – they must be gross by now."

"That's not what I'm talking about," said Cagney.

"Cagney?" said Aidan. "What have you done?"

Cagney looked sheepishly towards her bulging day-pack. "I might have accidentally stolen some snacks off the plane."

"That's alright," said Tess. "The snacks are for us to eat, they won't mind."

Cagney shuffled her feet.

Aidan studied his sister and sighed. "Okay, exactly *how* much food did you take?"

Cagney glanced at the flight attendant and lowered her voice. "Fifteen ham sandwiches, twelve Twinkies and thirty-two packets of peanuts."

"Whoa!" said Olivia.

"Impressive," said Tess.

"I'm worried I'm going to starve," Cagney said, defensively. "I hate Indian food – it does things to my insides."

"Ditch the sandwiches," said Aidan. "I don't think they'll care about the Twinkies and the peanuts."

Cagney stuffed two ham sandwiches in her mouth and dumped the rest into a nearby trash can.

"Yikes!" said Lissy, staring at the food bulging from Cagney's mouth. "You look like Tess."

The flight attendant headed towards the exit. "Your grandma left instructions to deliver you to a Miss Ishani Gupta."

The cousins threw on their backpacks, stepped through the doors, and took in the New Delhi airport. It was the noise Cagney first noticed, followed by the smell. A clamor assaulted her ears and a smell, unlike anything she'd smelled before, wafted up her nose. The difference a pair of doors could make was astounding. On one side all white and sterile. On the other, an instant immersion into Indian culture. Cagney rifled through her day-pack and brought out a ginormous packet of apple-scented tissues.

Airports were such happy places, thought Lissy, or at least they were in arrivals. Departures – probably not so much. She watched the throngs of people hug and kiss as they greeted long lost friends. Women in long colorful skirts and men with white cloth scarves around their heads mingled among people in shorts, tee-shirts and business suits. Yes, thought Lissy, if she was ever depressed she would go hang out in an airport arrivals lounge. That would soon cheer her up.

"So, where is she?" asked Cagney.

"I'm not sure," the flight attendant replied. "Your grandma said Miss Gupta would be here to meet you. Do you know what she looks like?"

Cagney removed her glasses and scowled.

The flight attendant took a step back. "I will take that as a no."

Fifteen minutes later there was still no sign of Miss Gupta and the flight attendant started to glance at her watch.

"Looks like I've acquired some children," she grinned. "I am taking you to the airline office. They can take it from here."

The cousins followed the flight attendant to a small glass cubicle. Opening the door, they piled into the room but promptly stopped. Behind the desk stood a small dark man wearing a white cloth hat and brandishing a bushy mustache. But that was not what the cousins were looking at. What they were looking at was a slim young woman with an incredibly long ponytail, who paced in front of the counter. She wore khaki pants and a polo shirt with a tiger embroidered on the collar. But the most interesting thing about her was she was yelling. She was yelling loudly.

"What do you mean, you don't know where they are? How can you have lost five children?" she asked, striding to and fro, her hair swishing like a mane behind her.

"But ma'am, I am knowing nothing about five children. Are you sure there are five of them?"

"Yes, you complete nincompoop. FIVE – SMALL – ITSY – BITSY – CHILDREN! Alone! In New Delhi, and you tell me you can't HELP me," she yelled. "Then, my little mustached friend, tell me this; if *you* can't help me, for the love of popcorn, tell me who can?"

"Miss Gupta, Ma'am?" whispered Lissy. "I think I might be able to help."

6

Miss Gupta's Babies

Miss Gupta was irate. Speeding through the airport, she made the flight attendant seem like she'd been dawdling. The cousins tore behind her, towards the exit and out into the heat of India.

"Children ... five of them ... like I have time ... with all I have to do ... can't believe my father ..."

Tess struggled for breath. "She's not exactly warm and cuddly, is she?"

"She's feisty," said Olivia.

"She's plain mad," said Cagney.

At once, Miss Gupta came to a stop. Crashing into one another, the cousins did a good impression of a deflating accordion. Whipping around Miss Gupta glared at Cagney.

"What did you call me?"

"Me?" squeaked Cagney. "I didn't say anything. Honest."

"Let me get something perfectly clear," said Miss Gupta. "I don't like children. I especially don't like *other* peoples' children, and I definitely don't like *five* children. You will be staying with me only until your grandma discovers ..."

"Discovers what?" said Olivia, her dimple deepening in her tanned face.

Miss Gupta glared. "Never you mind what she's discovering. The point is, you will *stay* out of the way. You will *not* interfere and you will speak *only* when spoken to. Is that clear?"

Aidan wiped away the sweat forming beneath his wavy hair. "Crystal."

Tess delved into Cagney's day-pack and ripped open one of the packets of peanuts. "When did you say we're going to see Grandma?"

Miss Gupta scrunched down and looked Tess square in the face.

"Peanut?" Tess asked, popping one into Miss Gupta's open mouth.

Miss Gupta gasped. Turning, she spat the nut into the air.

Unfortunately for Cagney, her nose was directly in its path. Cagney looked down cross eyed at the peanut stuck to the end of her nose. Mustering all possible dignity, she plucked the sticky substance from the end of her nose and tossed it into the trash.

"I'm allergic to peanuts!" explained Miss Gupta, not looking half as guilty as you would expect someone to look after spitting a nut in someone's face.

"Looks like you're down to the Twinkies," whispered Lissy.

Miss Gupta sighed. Standing, she glanced around. "Where on earth is Dinkar? The no good, useless, good for nothing ..."

"Who's Dinkar?" asked Tess.

Miss Gupta swung her long ponytail behind her. She bent down, her dark eyes level with Tess, although this time she kept her distance and eyed the peanuts suspiciously. "You're not getting that 'speak when you're spoken to' thing, are you?"

"Oh, I thought you were joking. You'll like us soon. Honestly, we can be very adorable."

The beep of a horn and squeal of tires broke Miss Gupta's gaze. "Finally," she sniffed, taking one last quizzical glance at Tess.

A large cream colored car rammed its front tire onto the curbside, making the cousins leap back in fear of losing their toes. It resembled a car that had once been fashionable – in say, 1950. Today there were a few dents and dings, but it was polished and clean, with an impressive tiger hood ornament shining proudly above the engine.

"Well, don't just stand there," barked Miss Gupta. "Get in."

Aidan threw their backpacks into the trunk while the girls piled inside. Squeezing in behind them he was happy to escape the wilting heat. Miss Gupta slid next to the driver, her cell phone to her ear and began bellowing into the mouth piece.

"What do you mean they're hiding? Well, go find them … Have you checked under the bed? What about the bath? You know they enjoy taking a bath. Oh, he's on top of the fridge? Then get him off … no I said off … OFF!"

"My goodness," said Lissy.

Pulling into traffic, the driver turned down the commentary on the radio and craned his body around towards the cousins before giving them a toothless grin. "I am Dinkar. It is very nice to be making your acquaintance."

Tess grinned back. "You too, Mr. Dinkar."

"You may call me Dinkar," said the driver, swerving to miss an oncoming bicycle. "Her babies," he said, nodding towards Miss Gupta. "She has four and is very protective. Even with a helper, she does not like to leave them for even a minute."

"Aaah, babies. My pink flowery hankie loves babies," said Tess.

"How old are they?" asked Cagney.

"They were born at the end of March," said Dinkar. "So they would be now three months old."

Lissy loved children, especially babies. She planned on having six and naming them after National Parks. Denali, Joshua, Sequoia, Zion and Bryce were all fine in Lissy's mind, although

Yosemite was a bit of a stretch. What the heck, unusual names built character.

With a blast of the horn the car lurched forward and Lissy came back to the present. "The nanny has lost four three-month-old babies?"

"No wonder she's in a bad mood," said Aidan.

"How on earth could a baby get on top of the fridge?" asked Olivia.

"Oh, this is nothing. Last week we found one in the oven."

"The oven!" exclaimed Tess.

"And the week before, they were swimming in the pool."

"Good grief," said Cagney. "I know babies are hard to look after, but that seems extreme."

"Yes ma'am, they are being very extreme," said Dinkar, grinning.

Dinkar was a thin man with dark brown skin and kind twinkling eyes. Scooting around, he jabbed a finger towards Olivia's blue baseball cap with a large red 'B' on the front. "Young man! You are a Red Sox fan?"

The cousins were used to people assuming Olivia was a boy. She dressed like a boy and acted like a boy. They'd given up correcting anyone. It just wasn't worth it.

Olivia's eyes lit up. "Aha."

"Big Papi," said Dinkar.

"He's so cool," said Olivia, whose autographed poster of Big Papi above her bed was one of her prized possessions.

"He is my hero." Dinkar pointed to a tattered picture of David Ortiz taped to his dashboard.

"Yikes!" said Cagney, noticing the unattended steering wheel.

Dinkar grinned a toothless smile and, leaning on the horn, steered the car away from several motorbikes.

The car dashboard was crowded with rectangular pictures. Small and faded, several were taped to the window, others pasted to the dashboard.

"Who are the pictures of?" asked Aidan.

"They are gods. Hindu gods. In India, we have gods for everything. This is Ganesha. He helps projects go smoothly." Dinkar pointed to a rather plump elephant. "Vishnu is the god of protection. He is especially helpful if you need to be saved. Siva is the god of destruction and Krishna the god of beauty. But it is Vishnu who comes in especially useful when driving."

"Why when driving?" asked Lissy.

Dinkar chuckled. "Because, little cousins, we are not very good drivers."

Cagney snapped a picture of three cows that had brought traffic to a snarling stop in the opposite lane. "Oh great!"

Dinkar grasped the crumpled picture of Vishnu and gave it a kiss. "Yes, I am hearing that we are having the most traffic accidents in the world."

"Excellent," said Aidan, checking for a non-existent seatbelt.

"But you do not have to worry. I am being a very good driver. Rarely am I having an accident. Of course there was that time…"

Dinkar continued to tell the cousins of several near misses and one almost fatality.

Lissy gave Spider a hug. "He's not exactly inspiring me with confidence," she whispered.

Aidan shut his eyes as a bicycle made for two, but carrying five, plus a cage of hedgehogs, wound its way in front of them.

"But luckily I only hit a lamppost, and the chicken managed to get away with barely a missing feather," said Dinkar, obviously proud of his ability to swerve from disaster.

Dinkar zig-zagged through the busy streets of New Delhi. New Delhi was the capital of India and the roads were broad and the buildings impressive. Traveling along the boulevard in either direction were hundreds of men on push bikes, a gazillion motorcycles and even a couple of water buffalo. How anything moved was a complete mystery.

Without warning Tess catapulted from her seat. Clonking her head on the window, she pointed down a side road. "Was that an elephant?" she gasped.

"Most likely," said Dinkar. "Sometimes when a couple gets married the elephant brings the groom to the wedding."

"Wow," said Tess. "India's magical."

Cagney tapped Miss Gupta on the shoulder. "Excuse me, but what *exactly* did you say our grandma's doing?"

Miss Gupta snapped her cell phone shut and scooted around to face Cagney. "For the love of hamsters, don't you people ever give up? How do I know what your grandma's doing? Probably up to her *usual* mischief."

Aidan raised an eyebrow. "Did you put the words 'grandma' and 'mischief' in the same sentence?"

"I told you, I don't know. Children don't need to know about serious stuff."

"We're not just stupid kids, you know," said Olivia.

"Oh, right, your grandma told me about that little problem you solved in Peru."

Cagney looked at Miss Gupta indignantly. "That was not a *little* problem. We found the lost treasure of the Inca."

"Yeah, sounds great," said Miss Gupta.

"It was lost for almost *five-hundred* years," said Lissy.

"All I know is, I'm stuck with five children whose grandma doesn't want them interfering. Think about it, kids; she obviously wants you as far away from the action as possible."

"There's action?" asked Olivia.

Miss Gupta ignored her.

"Great," said Cagney.

"Yeah," said Miss Gupta. "It's just fabulous."

With a blast of his horn, Dinkar swung the car left and zoomed under a brightly decorated arch.

Aidan glanced back at a multi-colored sign. "Dinkar, I thought we were going to stay with Miss Gupta?"

"You are," replied Dinkar.

Aidan slouched back into his seat. "Then why are you taking us to the zoo?"

7

Intruder

Dinkar bumped along a tree-lined avenue and pulled into a parking space. The car barely came to a stop before Miss Gupta threw open the door and jumped out.

Hurtling through a group of Japanese tourists, she tore past the zoo entrance, towards an ornate brick building. Fumbling at a key pad, she yanked on a handle and disappeared.

The cousins emerged into the heat and gazed in disbelief at the slowly closing door.

"Quick," said Dinkar. "You should be getting that before it closes."

Olivia raced to the door and shoved her foot in the opening. Peering around the corner she was just in time to see Miss Gupta hurry along a corridor before disappearing once more.

Aidan looked anxiously around. "I'm not sure about this. It looks kind of private."

Lissy watched as Dinkar swung the car around and, without a backward glance, bumped back down the avenue. "Were we supposed to follow her?"

"I guess," said Cagney. "What else are we going to do?"

Olivia jerked open the door and secured it with a rock. "Come on, it's only a building. There's nothing to be scared of."

The cousins hustled out of the heat, glad to feel the air-conditioning swirling around their ankles, and headed down a long, sterile passageway. Olivia stopped outside a purple door. "She went in here."

"Should we go in?" asked Tess.

"I don't think so," said Lissy. "Who knows what might be lurking behind that door?"

"It can't be *that* bad," said Aidan, "else Miss Gupta wouldn't have gone in."

Cagney put her hands on her hips and scowled. "Are you nuts? This is a zoo. Miss Gupta could be terrifying penguins, muskrats, even lions in there."

"She has a point," said Aidan.

Cagney nodded. "As I always like to say, curiosity killed the gnat."

"The gnat?" asked Lissy. "Don't you mean ..."

Cagney gave her a look.

"A gnat it is," said Lissy, who knew when to pick her battles.

"Well, we can't stay here," said Olivia. "I vote we take a chance."

"I'll tell you what," said Cagney. "Why don't *you* open the door. See what's inside, and if you're not mauled to a horrible death, we'll all go in."

"And if you are, we'll run like a six-legged llama," said Tess.

Cagney looked confused. "Sure, you crazy Chinese child."

Olivia cautiously eased the door open. First an inch, then another, and another. Slowly she poked her head around the door and gasped. Her dimple broke wide on her cheek as she smiled.

"Wow!" said Aidan, joining her.

Lissy nudged Aidan out the way and stuck her head around the opening. "In the name of Great Aunt Maud!"

The door swung on its hinges revealing Miss Gupta sitting on a rug cradling one of her babies. Another baby clambered up her back and two others played on the floor. The room was filled with children's toys, an entire miniature plastic kitchen lining one wall.

Miss Gupta did not look like the lady at the airport any more. She did not look mad. She did not look angry. An intense look of affection filled her smiling face as she gazed down and tickled a baby tiger under its chin.

"Come in, come in. Aren't they beautiful?" said Miss Gupta, rolling back and encouraging one of the baby tigers to jump on her belly.

"This explains a lot," said Aidan.

"What are their names?" asked Tess.

Miss Gupta pushed the tiger cub off her head and stood. "This one is Rhea. She's the most playful. That one over there is Raj. He's the biggest. Ravi is the quietest. He's kind of shy, and Rana, she likes to think she's the boss. Don't you Rana?"

"They're beautiful," said Lissy.

Olivia eyed Rana, who was busy chasing her tail. "Can we touch them?"

"Yes, but be careful. They are only babies, but they are still very strong. Rhea will give you a nip if she thinks she can get away with it."

Olivia made a bee-line for Rana, sinking to her knees and stroking her silky orange head. Aidan headed towards Raj. Lissy petted Ravi and Cagney snapped a picture of Rhea wrestling with Tess' purse.*

"They are Bengali tigers," said Miss Gupta.

Rhea let go of the pink fuzzy purse and Tess fell backwards landing bottom down, feet outstretched. Immediately Rhea started tussling with Tess' pink sparkly sandals.

"Are there different *types* of tigers?" asked Lissy, giggling as she watched Rhea lick Tess' toes.

*(Our friends at Whipsnade Zoo wanted us to tell you some information about tigers – please check the back of the book for more information).

"There are five different species. You can tell these are Bengali from the fringe around their face."

"How big will they get?" asked Aidan.

"Rhea and Rani will weigh up to 350 pounds. The boys may get as big as 500."

"Wow," said Lissy. "That's more than all of us put together."

"Yes. The tiger is the largest of all the cat family."

"Does India have a lot of tigers?" asked Olivia.

"Yes, we have more wild tigers than any other country," Miss Gupta said, proudly. "Tigers are at the top of the food chain. They only know one predator."

"What's that?" asked Aidan.

Miss Gupta shook her head, sadly. "Man. The tiger will soon become extinct. One hundred years ago, there were a 100,000 wild tigers, now less than 2,000 roam free. Three of the original eight species have died in the last seventy years."

"My goodness," said Lissy, "that's so sad."

"But why do people kill them?" asked Olivia.

"Several reasons," said Miss Gupta. "You can get a lot of money for a tiger."

Tess snuggled next to the playful Rhea. "How could anyone ever hurt you?"

"It's insane," said Aidan. "How could anyone kill something so beautiful?"

"People are poor," said Miss Gupta. "But it is no excuse. Soon the tiger will be hunted to extinction."

"Pardon me," came a high-pitched voice.

The cousins glanced up. A short, plump Asian man stood in the doorway behind them. He was dressed from neck to foot in a cream suit. Even his hat was cream, with a dash of scarlet around the band. Underneath the tightly buttoned suit glowed the hint of a bright pink shirt.

"It's Colonel Sanders," Cagney whispered to Olivia.

Olivia stifled a laugh. "Only if Colonel Sanders is Chinese."

"How did you get in here?" snapped Miss Gupta.

"The door was open," the man replied, with a sly smile.

Miss Gupta whipped around glaring at the cousins.

"For the love of toadstools, don't tell me you left the door open?"

Olivia stared miserably at the floor. "I'm sorry. I thought it closed."

Miss Gupta shook her head and ushered the man towards the door. "This is a private area. It is not open to the public."

A scowl flickered across the man's face. "I only want to see the cubs."

Miss Gupta put a hand on his cream jacket. "There is no viewing today," she insisted.

"Just a peek," said the man, sidestepping Miss Gupta and approaching Tess. Grasping Rhea by the scruff of her neck, the man held her up for inspection.

Tess looked on, helplessly.

"Okay, that's enough," said Miss Gupta.

Unexpectedly the man let out a scream of pain.

"Why you little ..." he cursed and flung Rhea across the room.

The cub landed on her bottom with a yelp.

"OUT!" screamed Miss Gupta.

The man looked at her with intense dislike and spat at her feet. "I see where they get their manners." Crossing to the door he let it slam behind him.

Lissy rushed to Tess, who was busy comforting Rhea. "Is she okay?"

"She's fine. Rhea's not going to let Pinky– hey!" shrieked Tess, as Miss Gupta pulled her up by her pink fuzzy tee-shirt.

"Out! Now!"

"Who me?" asked Tess. "What did I do?"

"Yes, you," Miss Gupta yelled. She wheeled around to face the others. "And you – and you too!"

Tess grabbed her purse and joined the charge towards the purple door.

"Wait!" Miss Gupta barked.

Nobody stopped.

"Okay, okay. Stop!"

One by one the cousins piled into the door.

"We *have* to stop doing this," said Cagney, her nose squished against the purple paint.

"Redeem yourselves," said Miss Gupta. "Go follow that slimy, good for nothing …" Miss Gupta paused and drew breath. "Just find out what he's up to, okay?"

Lissy gazed at her in disbelief. "Us?"

Miss Gupta reached towards them, her palms upturned. "Please, I cannot leave and I've seen that man before. I have a bad feeling about him. A really bad feeling."

8

Spying for Miss Gupta

The cousins dashed along the corridor and into the blinding heat.

"She's crazy," said Aidan.

"Ya think?" said Olivia.

"She's protective of her babies," said Lissy. "I can understand that."

"Yeah," said Tess. "My pink, fuzzy tee-shirt thinks she's okay."

"Your pink, fuzzy tee-shirt's out of its tiny little mind," said Olivia.

Lissy giggled.

"Well, you know what I mean," said Olivia, shaking her head.

"And she wants us to do what?" asked Cagney.

Tess pointed to the man in the cream suit striding along the tree-lined drive. "Follow Pinky."

"Why are you calling him Pinky?" asked Aidan.

"Did you see his outfit?" Tess tucked in her pink fuzzy tee-shirt. "Anyone who wears an outfit like that with a pink shirt is asking to be called Pinky."

Aidan studied his youngest cousin. From her fluorescent hair bands to her sparkly sandals, she was dressed entirely in luminous pink.

"Now there's the pot calling the kettle … er, pink," said Aidan.

Tess twirled her pigtail. "It's different for girls."

"She's as crazy as a kangaroo," said Cagney.

Tess stopped twirling and glanced at her oldest cousin.

Cagney shook her head. "Not you, although you definitely have your moments. I'm talking about Miss Gupta."

"I think you're right," said Olivia. "But do we want to risk upsetting her anymore?"

Lissy tossed her duffle bag over her shoulder. "I think we should do what she says."

"We haven't got anything else to do," said Aidan, watching Pinky head around the bend.

"Come on," said Olivia. "We'd better get a move on, or we're going to lose him."

"She's joking, right?" Cagney bent to tie a shoelace. "Right?" Cagney looked up to see everyone tearing down the avenue in a cloud of dust. She pushed her glasses onto the bridge of her nose, and mumbling something highly uncharitable, started after them.

At the end of the drive, the cousins clattered to a stop. Lissy scanned the crowded street. "Which way did he go?"

"There he is." Aidan pointed to a taxi on the opposite side of the road. Pinky's hat ducked inside and the door slammed.

"Oh great!" said Olivia. "We'll never be able to follow him now."

"Yes, we will," said Lissy.

Just in time, Olivia noticed the cream car heading straight for them. "Scatter!" she yelled.

The cousins leapt backwards as the car bounded onto the curb and screeched to a halt.

The window lowered and Dinkar stuck out his smiling face. "Hello, little cousins, have you seen the zoo already?"

Cagney wiped the sweat from her forehead. "We have a slight change of plans."

"Actually, we have a problem," said Aidan. "A huge problem."

"I am being good with problems." Dinkar jumped out from behind the driver's seat and threw open the rear door.

The cousins piled in, keeping an eye on the taxi as it pulled into the crowded street.

"Miss Gupta told us to follow someone," said Olivia.

"Follow who?" asked Dinkar.

"Follow that cab!" yelled Cagney.

Dinkar wheeled the car around and accelerated.

"Wait a sec," said Tess, confused. "That cab looks just like our car, but yellow."

"It's an Ambassador," said Olivia. "They're based on the English Morris Oxford."

Olivia was fascinated by cars, if she couldn't be a major league baseball star, then she wanted to design cars. Especially cars as cool as this one.

Dinkar glanced at Olivia. His eyebrows shot into his curly black hair, a beaming smile on his face. "Yes, your brother is right. They are often used as taxis. But this is an original from 1958." He patted the leather upholstery proudly.

With his hand placed firmly on the horn, Dinkar hurtled through the teeming streets. Turning right off the wide boulevard, Dinkar swerved into a narrower and, if possible, more crowded avenue.

"He is stopping by the market," cried Dinkar, waving his hands enthusiastically.

"Don't pull up behind him," said Olivia. "We don't want him to know we're following."

Dinkar passed the taxi and bounced onto the sidewalk behind a befuddled cow.

"Yes, yes, I have been watching many James Bond movies. I am knowing exactly what to do. I am your get-away driver, right?"

"Right, Dinkar," said Aidan, smiling.

"I will wait right here for you. Agent Dinkar at your service."

"Quick," said Olivia, "or we'll lose him."

The cousins stumbled out of the car and hurried to the entrance of the market. Grinding to a halt, they stopped and stared.

Cagney raised her camera and fired off a couple of pictures. "It's not exactly Target, is it?"

The narrow alleyway contained a market, riotous with color. Women wrapped in flowing silks sat cross-legged on blankets. Vegetables the cousins could not name, tumbled from waist high sacks around them. Shops bursting with pots and pans, shoes and radios, snaked into the distance.

Pinky disappeared behind a plump man with four chickens squawking around his neck.

Olivia grabbed Cagney's hand and dragged her into the alley. "Come on!"

"Wow, I want what she's wearing." Tess pointed to a woman wearing a sapphire fitted top with a matching long skirt.

Lissy gave the woman an admiring glance, as she dashed past. "She's wearing a sari. Spider says saris are traditional Indian dress for women."

Sprinting to keep up with Olivia, Aidan pointed to a man who wore a long shirt and matching pants. "What about those?"

Lissy gulped in a breath of humidity. "They're called kurta pajamas."

"The men wear their pajamas in public?" asked Cagney, brushing by a man holding a bottled snake.

Lissy averted her eyes from an animal being roasted on a spit. "Nope. They're not really pajamas. Like the sari, it's traditional Indian dress."

Aidan eyed his own damp tee as he wiped the sweat from his brow. "It sure looks comfortable."

"Pajamas is an Indian word," said Lissy, who now not only huffed, but puffed as well. "His cloth hat is called a turban."

"You don't say!" Olivia was stunned by her cousins' sudden interest in fashion. "Move it guys, or we're going to lose him."

Lissy had a stitch. She didn't like running at the best of times, plus the smell of the market was making her slightly sick. "What shall we do if he turns around?"

"Duck," said Tess.

"Good idea," said Aidan.

"No really! Duck!" yelled Tess, as a ball of screaming red hurtled towards them.

9

Into the Market

Olivia scooped down and seized the red, hand-sized ball that had landed inches from her feet. "Okay, who's the wise guy throwing a ball in the middle of a crowded market?"

"Up here," came a voice.

Olivia looked skyward. Several young boys peered over the edge of a flat topped roof.

"Be a sport," said the tallest. He clapped his hands and held them out, face up.

"What do you mean 'be a sport'?" said Olivia. "You nearly killed me."

"That would have been very bad luck," said one of the younger boys.

"But you are fine," said another, "so, can we have our ball, please?"

Tess squinted into the afternoon sun. "What are you doing up there?"

The boys grinned at each other, as if Tess had asked the stupidest question in the world.

"We are playing cricket of course," the tallest one said, a large white grin breaking across his dark face.

Cagney took off her glasses and cleaned them. "On a rooftop?"

"There are no parks around here," said the tiniest.

Olivia sighed. "Oh, all right." She aimed the ball towards the young boy, tossing it into the air. "But you should be careful. If you fall, you could break a leg."

Cagney smirked.

"Well!" Olivia shrugged. "They could."

"Come on," said Aidan. "We have a job to do."

The cousins continued into the market. Vendors took up a sizable chunk of where the sidewalk should have been and shoppers took up the rest. Holding hands, the cousins snaked their way through the bustling alleyway.

"Can you see him?" asked Lissy.

"Lucky for us, that hat makes him easy to spot," said Olivia.

"Duck!" cried Cagney.

Lissy looked around anxiously. "Not another ball?"

"Nope, he's doubling back!" said Cagney.

The cousins fell to their knees in front of a rather surprised elderly man. The man was surrounded by burlap sacks full of spices. He sat bare footed and cross legged, and on his right shoulder he balanced an ancient radio.

"Saffron?" the man asked, reluctantly lowering the radio and standing it on a blanket.

"Ooh, yes please." Tess nodded her head before turning to Aidan. "What's saffron?" she whispered.

Lissy pointed towards a sack full of orange reddish flakes. "It's an Indian spice."

Tess leaned towards the bag and inhaled deeply. Choking and sputtering she sprung back. "Maybe not," she gasped.

"We'll have a pound," said Olivia, ignoring her sister as Lissy pounded Tess between the shoulders.

The old man's eyes lit up, as he rose to his feet.

"Maybe that's too much," said Lissy. "I think saffron's really expensive."

"No, no," said Cagney, as an enormous paper bag was produced.

The man stopped. "You do not want a pound?"

Aidan grabbed a much smaller bag and handed it to the disappointed man. "So sorry. Maybe just *this* much?"

Cagney counted out her rupees and placed the colorful notes in the saffron man's wrinkled palm.

"Actually that was really cheap," said Aidan, doing the math in his head. "Things in India are a bargain."

Cagney tossed the bag to Olivia. "Here."

"I don't want it," said Olivia, flinging it back.

"You asked for it." Cagney shoved the saffron into Olivia's hands.

"Only for a decoy," said Olivia, launching it back.

"Give it to me." Aidan grabbed the saffron and stuffed the paper bag into his day-pack.

"Do you think we could find Pinky now?" asked Lissy.

"Good idea," said Tess. "Where'd he go?"

In the commotion, Aidan realized they'd completely forgotten to watch where Pinky was heading. The alleyway split in two, and he had no idea which fork he'd taken. "Olivia, climb that pole. Maybe you'll be able to see him if you're higher up."

"I have a better idea." Olivia twisted Aidan around and scampered up his back. Seconds later she was perched on his shoulders. She now stood at least a head higher than everyone else, and had a clear view into the two alleyways.

Aidan took a deep breath and counted to ten. He got all the way to twenty before stopping for breath, trying desperately not to imagine what clung to the bottom of Olivia's sneakers.

"I don't see him."

"Great! I can't believe you've lost him already," said Cagney. "Some spies you are."

"We haven't lost him." Lissy lowered her voice. "He's behind us."

Pinky emerged from a colorful candy store, popping a round red candy into his mouth and crunching down hard. Within seconds he was ploughing his way through the throng of people.

Olivia sprung to the ground. "Quick, get down."

Once more the cousins came face to face with the saffron man. He again lowered the radio, which blared out an agitated commentary.

"More?" the old man asked, hopefully.

Cagney crouched low. "No!"

"Thank you," added Lissy, with an apologetic smile.

Olivia and Tess blended well into the dark-haired crowd, but Cagney, Aidan and Lissy stuck out like a bikini at Thanksgiving.

Pinky passed behind the cousins, his legs brushing Lissy's back. Lissy let out a squeak, but Pinky did not look down, popping another candy into his mouth before disappearing into the alley to his right.

"Okay, let's try not to lose him this time," said Olivia, scrambling to her feet.

The cousins inched their way through the shoppers, the flash of cream in front of them indicating they were still heading in the right direction. They kept close behind him as he wound his way through the market's twisting maze. At a T-junction Pinky took a left. Cagney stopped and peered into the gloom. This alleyway was narrower and much darker. It smelled musty and there were far fewer people.

"What's wrong?" asked Olivia.

"I'm not sure," said Cagney. "But something is."

10

The Death of the King

Lissy gazed into the dark alley. "I don't know if I want to go down there."

"Me neither," said Tess. "My pink polka-dot shorts don't think it's a good idea."

"A rustling movement behind them made Cagney leap in fright. "Was that a rat?" Cagney pointed towards the gutter.

"Of course not," said Olivia, not even looking. "Just a very small cat."

Cagney gave her a scathing look. Olivia gave her one back.

"Are we going to follow Pinky or not?" asked Aidan.

"Not me," said Cagney.

Tess looked eagerly at several vibrantly colored saris hanging for sale from a doorway.

"You like?" asked a young girl, emerging from the store.

Cagney ran her hand down the exquisite material. It felt like the softest cream.

"I have special for you," the young girl added, a cheeky grin on her pale brown face.

"I think we might wait here for you," said Lissy, as the shop girl draped the palest green silk around her arms.

"I'm sure I'd just get in your way," said Tess, disappearing into the store.

"Yeah!" said Cagney. "The basketball is most definitely in your court."

"Then you guys stay here and we'll be ..." Olivia stopped, the girls were gone. "Puh!"

Aidan squeezed Olivia's hand. "Come on, we'll be fine."

Olivia and Aidan crept into the dank, musty alleyway.

"Are you nervous?" asked Olivia.

"Are you?"

Olivia stole a look over her shoulder. "Nah."

Aidan forced a smile. "Course! Me neither."

Olivia and Aidan continued down the darkened path. Gone were the exotic colors and smells. In their place came a dampness and stench neither wanted to name.

"Spices?" said a dark, ragged voice from an even darker doorway.

"No thanks," said Aidan, hurrying on.

The cousins passed dirt-encrusted windows and doorways that owned no doors. Two small children leaned in an archway, their eyes liquid brown, smudges of grime around their mouths. They gazed shyly at the two cousins and Olivia smiled, not looking where she was walked.

Turning forward, she gasped, coming nose to scalp with an ancient man bent almost double. He peered at her with hollow eyes. His breath rancid, his clothes limp around his bony body.

"Rupees?" he croaked.

Olivia backed away.

"I think he wants money," said Aidan, putting himself between the man and Olivia.

"I'm sorry," said Olivia. "Not right now."

"Rupees?" he repeated. His scrawny fingers grasping Aidan's wrist.

Aidan edged around the man. "I'm sorry, but this really isn't a good time."

Olivia felt a hand on her arm, then another and another. Within seconds they were completely surrounded by men dressed in rags.

"I don't have anything," she implored, stumbling after her Red Sox cap, which had been knocked into the gutter.

Aidan sunk to the ground and rifled through his day-pack. Standing, he launched a small brown package down the alley. "Take this."

Hastily the hands broke loose and the beggars shuffled along the alley after the offering.

"Quick," said Aidan.

But Olivia was ahead of him, already sprinting in the opposite direction.

Chasing behind her, Aidan caught her arm. Olivia spun around and with a flying leap, kicked him in the stomach. "I said no!"

Aidan tumbled backwards and slid down the wall.

"Oops!" said Olivia.

Aidan lay slumped in an open drain, a bemused look on his face. "I'm alright," he said, shaking his head. "But you're dangerous."

"I'm prepared," said Olivia, offering him a hand. "What did you throw?"

Aidan staggered to his feet and wiped the dirt from his shorts. "Half a pound of saffron."

The beggars behind them, Olivia and Aidan continued down the alley. The bustling market seemed far away and all was quiet, as the two cousins inched along the filthy passageway.

Ahead, Pinky's cream suit could barely be seen in the gloom. However, just when Olivia thought the alley would go on forever, Pinky hopped up three crumbling steps and disappeared behind a long frayed curtain.

The two cousins cautiously approached the entryway. Two massive pots stood guard either side of the door. Behind the urns, were two grubby windows containing a jumble of jars.

"What type of shop is *that?*" Olivia pointed to a grimy sign that was definitely not English.

"I don't know, but I'll copy it and see if I can figure it out with my *Scribbling Sanskrit* book."

Taking a pencil and notebook out of his day-pack, Aidan carefully copied the strange looking squiggles. "Now what?"

"I guess it wouldn't hurt to get a bit closer," said Olivia.

The alleyway was not completely deserted, but it didn't give the cousins anywhere to hide should Pinky re-appear.

"Let's hide behind those." Aidan darted towards the two massive earthenware pots standing either side of the doorway.

Olivia hurried towards the ragged curtain. "We'll be seen. Better get in."

Aidan peered into the pot and checked it for grossness. Not seeing anything too disgusting, he crawled onto the rim and lowered himself inside. Immediately he heard raised voices: Pinky's, shrill and high pitched, the other voice, much lower and older.

"So," said the older man, "what is your plan?"

"In three days you will have him," squeaked Pinky.

"Are you positive?"

"Yes. Everything is in place. My colleagues have been working for months. Nobody suspects a thing."

"How can you be so sure?" the older voice asked.

"It is a fail-safe plan, but just in case I am being watched, I am going to Agra. What could be more normal than to visit the most famous site in India?"

"Very good," replied the old voice.

"Once I have done some sightseeing, I will re-board the train, and by morning we will be ready."

"You are sure everything is in place?"

"Yes," squeaked Pinky. "I will supervise every last detail. Do not worry. You will have your King in China by the weekend."

"And he will be dead?" the old man asked.

"As a dodo!"

Olivia and Aidan heard the curtain swish and Pinky's feet stride down the steps. Admiring his reflection in the grimy window he adjusted his cream hat and popped another candy into his mouth. Olivia's legs started to cramp. She longed to stand and dispose of whatever was climbing her leg. Aidan felt the same. Carefully he shifted position and ever so slightly the pot rocked.

Pinky spun to face Aidan's pot gazing suspiciously at the open lid. Slowly, Pinky began to move closer. Aidan crouched lower and seriously considered whether his heart was going to explode.

Suddenly, a bedraggled cat shot from behind the earthenware pot. What was left of its fur spiked into the air and, drawing back its lips, it hissed ominously at Pinky, before scuttling down the alleyway.

Pinky leapt backwards, lost his footing and landed smack dang on top of Olivia's pot. Olivia, rocked by the impact, peered up to find Pinky's cream bottom filling the opening. Resisting the urge to poke it, she concentrated instead on hoping the pot wouldn't shatter. Pinky staggered off the urn and re-arranged his crumpled suit.

"I hate cats," he said chuckling, and spat into the pot on the left before striding back along the alleyway. Waiting several seconds, Olivia and Aidan slowly rose.

"He sat on me," said Olivia.

"Count yourself lucky," said Aidan, swiping drool off his tee. "He spat on me!"

Olivia, bit her lower lip in an effort to seem sympathetic, but it was no good – that darn dimple gave her away every time. "Gross! No really it is."

Pinky paced down the passageway and headed around the corner.

"Quick," said Olivia. "We mustn't lose him."

Aidan and Olivia toppled out of the pots and tore along the alleyway in search of Pinky – a man about to commit murder.

11

The Bus Ride

Olivia and Aidan emerged from the passageway and tore towards the three girls.

"Come on," said Aidan.

"Now?" asked Tess, who was wrapped in a pink sari and busy admiring herself in a dusty mirror. "But I bought shiny bangles and look, they're pink!"

Olivia grabbed the end of the sari and pulled. "Right now."

Tess spun like a top, as the flowing material fell from her body.

"Did you know the silk produced in India is the finest in the world?" said Lissy.

Olivia dumped the sari in the hands of the startled shop girl. "I do now."

Aidan grasped Lissy's hand and herded her out the store. "Come on. We'll tell you everything on the way."

The cousins plowed through the market, keeping Pinky just within their view. Quickly Aidan told the girls what they'd heard.

"Oh no!" said Tess. "That's dreadful."

"What should we do?" asked Lissy.

"I'm not sure," said Olivia, "but we must find out where Pinky's staying and, if possible, his real name."

The cousins emerged from the alleyway hot, sticky and not exactly looking their best.

Lissy scanned the crowded street. "Where's Dinkar?"

Dinkar and the Ambassador were gone. They had disappeared. And furthermore, they were not there.

"Oh, what a shame," said Cagney, wiping Lord knows what from her forehead. "But on the plus side, we can give up chasing a murderer and finish shopping." Cagney spun around and started back towards the sari shop.

"Not so fast!" Olivia grabbed the back of Cagney's dress and jerked her to a sudden stop. She pointed across the road. "Pinky's right there."

"What's he waiting for?" asked Tess.

Aidan saw a disheveled looking bus come rumbling around the corner. "Of course, he's waiting for the bus."

Olivia tore across the road, beckoning the others to follow. "Quick!"

Aidan grabbed his sister's hand. "Come on, slow poke."

"Gross, Aidan. You're sopping wet."

"It's the heat," said Aidan. "I'm wilting faster than a Texas salad."

Cagney snatched her hand away and moved briskly across the road. The others were already clambering up the steps.

It was a bus unlike anything Cagney had ever seen. The dirt so thick, Cagney could barely see the red and yellow paint below. She watched the people jostle to cram themselves into its filthy interior and wished, for the thousandth time that day, to be in Texas, preferably at the mall.

Olivia took another step upward, but before she could go any farther her path was blocked by a bright purple sari. Olivia glanced up to see who the sari belonged to and found her entry barred by an elderly woman with a red dash of paint between her eyes and a huge gold hoop circling from her nose.

"No, no!" she said, waving her wrinkled hands in a shooing motion.

Olivia bounced back onto the sidewalk. "What do you mean, 'no'?"

"Full. We are full."

The bus was indeed full. It practically bulged. Olivia observed people hanging out of windows and an aisle overflowing with a flock of school girls.

"Only room on top."

Tess looked up. "On top of what?"

The woman jabbed her hand upwards, a cascade of golden bangles tumbling down her arm, before turning and melting into the crowd.

A trickle of passengers edged along the side of the bus.

"This way." Aidan hurried to the rear, then stopped dead. Snaking up the back was a ladder. A ladder that clung to the bus by several rusty bolts and sheer determination.

"No way!" said Cagney.

"They're joking, right?" said Lissy.

"Come on," said Olivia, "It'll be fun."

Cagney watched her cousin nimbly climb the metal ladder. "Olivia, come back this instant."

"Whoa!" squeaked Olivia, as she was lifted on top of the bus by a swarm of outstretched hands.

"Good grief," said Cagney.

Lissy shook her head. "This is not going to end well."

"Don't worry," said Tess. "My pink fluffy purse has a good feeling about this."

Two sharp bangs on the side of the bus were obviously the sign to get moving. The bus began to blow gray gusts of smoke as its engine cranked into gear. Lissy leapt onto the ladder and scrambled up. She too was grabbed and hoisted over the edge. Tess came right behind her.

Aidan stepped onto the bottom rung as the bus jerked forward. "Come on, Cagney."

Cagney stood there, arms across her dress, a defiant look on her face.

"Cagney, run!" pleaded Aidan, as the bus chugged into the noisy street.

Cagney did not move.

Aidan sprung from the moving bus and hurried to his sister. Grabbing her wrist, he half pulled, half dragged her forwards.

"I can't," said Cagney. "You know I'm terrified of heights!"

"You can do it, sis – I'll be right behind you."

Cagney reached the ladder and stepped onto the bottom rung. Tentatively she climbed three steps before a yelp told Aidan she too had been heaved onto the roof. Running to keep up, Aidan launched himself at the ladder and scampered skyward.

The top of the bus was as crowded as below. Old men, young women and three goats, all jostled for position on the broad ceiling. Aidan was helped over the edge by a strong teenager with an engaging smile.

"Thanks," said Aidan.

"No problem," said the boy.

Aidan searched the crowd for his cousins. There, at the front, sat Olivia, her legs dangling over the edge, the wind blowing her short dark hair. Behind her were Tess and Lissy, perched safely between three older women. But where was Cagney? Peering down he saw a mass of curls blowing gently in the breeze. Cagney lay face down on the bus, her fists clenched around the pajama clad legs of two teenage boys.

"Cagney, are you okay?"

"Just tell me when it's time to get off," she said, not looking up and re-establishing a tighter grip on the bemused boys' ankles.

"It's her first time," explained Aidan.

The teenagers shrugged and motioned for Aidan to step around them. Aidan squeezed through the passengers until he reached the front. Plopping down next to Olivia, he swung his legs over the front, grabbing her arm to steady himself as the bus hit a pot hole.

Olivia's face was bronzed, her wide brown eyes glowed in the afternoon sun. Aidan had a rush of fondness for his closest cousin, as he realized just how much she was enjoying herself.

Olivia turned to face him. Her dimple deep, her face cracked into a smile. "Don't you just love India?"

Aidan gave it some thought. There they were, halfway around the world, not an adult in sight, and all five of them on top of a rickety bus, holding on for dear life as they chased an unknown Chinese man across New Delhi. Aidan grinned back at his cousin. Yes, there was no doubt in his mind. Aidan absolutely *loved* India.

12

The Wedding Party

Soon all traces of the bustling market place were left behind, replaced instead with grand buildings and green parks. It was hard to believe it was the same city, thought Aidan, as the remnants of colonial India rose to greet them.

At each stop, Olivia leaned over the edge and watched to see if Pinky got off. Finally, hidden in a swarm of school children, she saw the distinctive cream hat bob onto the street.

"Quick," said Olivia.

She and Aidan staggered to their feet and, tottering down the bus, found Lissy and Tess, chatting with three colorfully dressed women.

Aidan gave Tess' pigtail a playful tug. "Come on, he's getting off."

Tess and Lissy stumbled to their feet and followed Olivia across the already swaying bus.

"Where's Cagney?" asked Lissy.

"I'm here," came a muffled voice.

Tess looked down. "Where?"

"Underneath the chicken," said Cagney.

While Olivia and Aidan were at the front of the bus, an old woman, with six flapping birds, had positioned herself next to Cagney. During the journey a plump brown hen had found a resting place amongst Cagney's curly locks.

Olivia picked up the chicken and handed it to the woman. "For goodness sake," she said, hoisting Cagney to her feet.

The bus lurched forward and the cousins teetered towards the edge. The bus picked up speed and the five clung to each other, as they bumped along the boulevard. As soon as the bus squealed to a stop Olivia whisked down the ladder, followed by Lissy and Tess.

"Come on, Cagney." cried Olivia, peering anxiously down the street with the glim hope of spotting a band of scarlet.

"She's coming," said a voice from above.

"Is that who I think it is?" asked Tess, as one of the teenage boys appeared at the top of the ladder with a pair of struggling legs flung over his shoulder.

"I can't bear to look," said Lissy, covering her eyes.

Olivia left her eyes open but covered her mouth, afraid of what might come out.

"Good thing she has clean underwear on. Right, Olivia?" said Tess.

Olivia nodded, still unable to speak, wishing with all her might she had a camera.

Her dress blowing high in the wind, her feet kicking in protest, Cagney was lowered over the side of the bus. The teenager stumbled down the ladder before dropping her, bottom first, onto the sidewalk.

Cagney plucked a chicken feather from her curls before inhaling a large breath. "And you can wipe that dimple off your face," she muttered, glaring at Olivia.

Olivia tried, but knew her limitations.

Aidan tumbled down the ladder, leaping off the last two rungs as the bus lurched once more into traffic. "Thanks!" he said to the teenager.

"Not a problem," said the boy, giving Aidan a high five before turning and melting into the crowd.

"What are we going to do?" asked Tess, reaching down and helping Cagney to her feet.

"Let's head to the last bus stop," said Olivia, who'd finally stopped smirking.

"Yeah," said Aidan, "it isn't too far, maybe we'll find him."

The cousins turned and headed along the boulevard. Looking behind them, Cagney let out a shriek.

"What is it?" asked Lissy.

"It's a … it's a …"

"It's Jumbo," said Tess.

Out of a side street, a jumble of men came running towards them. In the middle plodded an elaborately decorated elephant. Abruptly, the cousins were consumed by the crowd. Jostled along the street, they couldn't help but stumble along with the parade.

Tess bounded alongside the elephant. "What's going on?"

"Wedding," shouted one of the men.

"Oooh, how fun. I love weddings."

"Tess! Where are you?" yelled Olivia.

"Over here. It's a wedding procession. Can we go?"

Olivia smushed her hands over her ears as a smattering of firecrackers pierced the air. "It doesn't seem like we have much choice," she said, grabbing her sister's hand in an effort to stay together. "Where are the others?"

"I'm not sure. The minute Jumbo appeared we got separated."

The crowd turned a corner and swept the sisters along in its wake.

"This is crazy. We're never going to find Pinky at this rate," said Olivia.

"Ooh, look," said Tess, glancing upwards.

Olivia peered at the great beast thundering along beside her. On top of the elephant sat a dignified man, wearing a long gold coat with matching gold pants. On his head he wore an intricate golden hat with a fan sticking out one side. But it was not the elaborate clothes that caught Olivia's eye. It was the boy sitting in front of him in the red tee. It was Aidan.

13

Aidan Hitches a Ride

Olivia was not often stunned, but she let this be an exception. "Aidan! What are you doing?"

The elephant was not very comfortable and his hair was really prickly against Aidan's bare legs, but the view was incredible. Aidan wished his friends at school could see him. He felt like a modern-day Hannibal, except for the whole alps thing. Aidan might not have been a mighty warrior, but he sure felt like one.

Looking down, he spotted Cagney and Lissy's light brown hair bobbing along in a wave of ebony.

"Cagney!" shouted Olivia.

Cagney's frazzled hair bounced up and down, a stray chicken feather working itself loose, as she raced to keep up with the crowd. Cagney turned and almost got trampled in the process. "Can't … stop."

"Keep going," yelled Olivia. "They can't keep up this pace for much longer."

"Where's Aidan?" asked Lissy, anxiously.

Tess and Olivia glanced at each other.

"You don't want to know," said Olivia.

The girls charged along the road with the richly painted elephant lumbering by their side. Finally the crowd that had surrounded them like a raging river, slowed to a trot. Sweaty and exhausted, they came to a halt.

"Oh thank goodness," said Lissy, panting for breath. "I was afraid I'd get flattened if I stopped."

Cagney bent double with exertion. "Where did you say Aidan was?"

Before Olivia had a chance to answer, the enormous beast sunk to its knees, raised its trunk and let forth an ear shattering bellow.

Cagney stuck her fingers in her ears. "I suppose he thinks that's funny." Cagney glared at Jumbo, who did seem to have a smile on his leathery face.

Cagney's mouth dropped. "Is that?" she asked, pointing up.

"Yep," said Tess.

Aidan scampered past the elephant's ear, onto its knee, and finally, with a thud, his sneakers hit the ground.

Cagney bent double and watched another chicken feather float slowly to the ground. "How did you … what did you … who put you …?"

Aidan grinned at the four girls. "That was great."

No one answered. Aidan was about to say something else but thought better of it. The girls, hunched over and clutching their sides, did not look their best. In fact, they'd rarely looked worse. A sweaty, exhausted mess was how Aidan would describe them. Luckily, a highly developed sense of survival told him descriptions were probably best avoided right now. Perspiration soaked their already damp clothes and the distinctive smell of chicken filled the air. Yeah, Aidan decided to remain very silent.

"It's just … not … fair." Cagney re-adjusted her glasses and watched as several men clapped Aidan on the back. With a deafening trumpet, the elephant rose to his feet and strode into the nearby park.

"Apparently, it's good luck to have a young boy accompany the groom on the way to his wedding," said Aidan. "The next thing I knew I was in the clouds."

Cagney sank onto a nearby bench and let out an ominous growl.

The wedding party had deposited the cousins by the side of a beautifully landscaped garden. An overflowing bus ambled up and a gaggle of school children jumped off.

"Hey," said Olivia. "This is where Pinky got off."

"Are you sure?" asked Lissy.

"Quite sure," said Olivia. "Those girls are wearing the same uniforms as the girls who got off with him.

"Which way do you think he went?" asked Aidan.

"Oh, come on." Cagney dragged a crumpled tissue from her pocket and mopped her crimson face. "He could be anywhere by now."

Olivia scrambled up a lamp post and scanned the surrounding area. Slithering back down, she gave it a kick. "Cagney's right. It's hopeless. He's nowhere to be seen."

"You mean I showed my underwear to half of New Delhi for nothing?" said Cagney. "Great! Just great."

"What's going on over there?" Lissy pointed to a group clustered by the gate of the park. A reedy melody floated out of the crowd.

"Ooh! A band!" Tess took off towards them.

"Come on, let's go take some pictures," said Aidan, happy to change the subject.

Aidan hauled his disgruntled sister to her feet and crossed to the growing cluster of people. Peeking through the crowd, Aidan could see a leathery skinned man sitting cross legged on the grass. He was robed in shabby white, and in front of him sat a tall oval basket. In his bony fingers he grasped a narrow wooden instrument with a bulge at one end. The music floated towards them, and Tess, who had nudged her way to the front, was dancing.

Tess reached in the pocket of her pink polka-dot shorts. Finding several rupees she approached the musician and dropped the coins into the basket. Immediately Tess let out a blood-curdling scream.

Aidan and Olivia fought their way through the crowd to see Tess standing inches from the basket, transfixed. Her hands clasped her cheeks. Her mouth hung open. Tess stood nose to fang with a large Indian cobra who swayed in time to the music.

Olivia grabbed her sister and dragged her through the crowd. "It's only a snake. You're not scared of snakes are you?"

"Of course not; I love Hiss. It was just the shock. Who on earth carries a dancing snake around with them?"

Lissy wrapped her arms around Tess. "A snake charmer?"

A loud beep and the next thing Lissy knew, Tess was quite literally in her arms. Legs wrapped around her waist. Head buried amongst her curls.

Cagney almost dropped her camera. "That darn elephant."

"It's not Jumbo," said Lissy, locking eyes with Olivia. "It's Dinkar."

"Scatter," cried Olivia.

Everyone leapt backwards as Dinkar careened the Ambassador onto the curb and squealed to a halt.

"Hello, little cousins."

"Dinkar!" cried Tess, squirming from Lissy's arms and sprinting towards the car.

"Where were you?" asked Olivia.

"I am sorry, little cousins, but I went to my uncle's store to listen to the test match."

"The what?" asked Aidan.

"India versus Pakistan," said Dinkar.

"What *about* India and Pakistan?" said Cagney.

"Cricket!" explained Dinkar. "It is our most popular sport. When India plays Pakistan, the whole of India listens."

"And the whole of Pakistan?" asked Olivia.

"Puh!" said Dinkar, dismissively.

"Who's winning?" asked Tess.

Dinkar scowled. "Don't ask."

"How did you find us?" asked Lissy.

"I was arriving at the marketplace as you were hopping on the bus. I followed and saw you running with that rather splendid elephant."

Aidan grinned, and gave Dinkar a high-five through the open window.

"But why are you not with your Chinaman?" asked Dinkar.

"We lost him," said Lissy, glumly.

"But he is at the hotel," said Dinkar, stepping out of the Ambassador.

"What hotel?" asked Olivia.

"The Royal Grenadier." Dinkar pointed towards an ornate brick building. "I saw him waddling up the steps like an albino penguin."

Tess flung her arms around the startled man. "Dinkar, you're the best."

Dinkar broke into a toothless grin. "Yes, yes, little cousin. Who is being the James Bond now?"

*
* *

14

The Royal Grenadier

Olivia dashed across the road and bounded up the steps of the ornate building. A young man sat hunched on a stool by the front door, a radio at his feet. As the cousins hurtled by, he jumped to attention and swung the door wide for the five to enter. The blast of air was as refreshing as a summer shower in Texas.

"That feels so good." Tess twirled into the foyer. "My pink stripy socks are desperate for some chilly air."

The lobby was opulent and reminded Lissy of a time gone by. To their right, a gracious marble staircase swept to the second floor. To their left, a solid mahogany desk stood unmanned. In the middle of the lobby were four ornate columns and several serious pots containing a multitude of greenery. Scattered between the columns were several very comfortable looking armchairs. Lissy sunk into one, and the others followed.

Tess slumped into the plush chair and stretched her toes. "This is more like it."

"But where is everyone?" asked Olivia.

Aidan glanced around. Not a soul could be seen. No guests, no hotel staff, not even the ding of an old fashioned elevator. "I don't know."

"It's like the Mary Celeste," said Lissy.

Cagney looked up from cleaning the grime from her glasses.

"You know," said Lissy, "the ghost ship found adrift with nobody on it."

"We know what it is," said Aidan. "This is just not the time to be reminded of it."

Olivia sprang from her chair and approached the desk. "Hello? Anybody here?"

A sudden cheer erupted. Olivia stumbled back in surprise, as a head, bald as a tea-cup, emerged from behind the counter. "Er, hello?"

"Good day, good day," said a wiry looking man with round green glasses. "And how may I be assisting you?"

"We wondered where everyone was?"

"Was?" The desk clerk beamed at her. "My dear boy, everyone is listening to the test match."

"Of course," said Olivia. "India vs. Pakistan."

The desk clerk rubbed his hands together with glee. "Precisely."

"And did India just score a goal?"

The desk clerk's brow wrinkled. "Not a goal, a run. Seven runs to be precise and four wickets." And, with an imaginary bat in his hand, he swung low, smacking an equally imaginary ball.

"Well that's all right then." Olivia turned back towards the lobby.

"Would you be liking some chai?" asked the desk clerk.

"Chai?" said Olivia, surprised.

The desk clerk glanced at the ornate clock standing behind him. The large hand clicked to the top and four somber gongs rang out.

"Goodness gracious yes," said the desk clerk. "It is most definitely chai-time."

"Er, … then I guess we will."

The desk clerk seized a bell and wobbled it vigorously. "Yash will be right with you," he said, taking aim with the invisible cricket bat once more.

Olivia skidded across the slick marble floor and hurled herself into her chair.

"So?" said Cagney.

"Cricket." Olivia shrugged, as if that was enough of an explanation.

"So, what's the plan?" asked Aidan.

"Apparently we're having chai with someone named Yash."

"Chai?" said Aidan.

"It's a type of tea," said Lissy. "But who's Yash?"

"I am Yash," came a nervous voice from behind a pot plant.

Lissy turned to see a boy, not much older than Cagney, in a black and gray uniform easily two sizes too big for him. "Wow, they start working young here." She gave the boy a kindly smile.

"I think we're going to have some chai," said Lissy.

Yash fiddled nervously with his gold buttons. "Ma'am?"

"Tea." said Tess, assuming the 'I'm a little tea-pot' position, ready to tip and pour.

Yash gave a small bow. "Yes ma'am, but what kind of tea?"

"Hot tea," suggested Lissy.

"I mean what *type* of tea?"

"There are different types?" asked Cagney.

Yash cowered even lower. "Yes ma'am, this is India, we produce the most tea in the world."

"More than China?" asked Olivia.

"Yes ma'am. We have Assam, Darjeeling, Nilgiri and, of course, Chai ..."

"I'll take a bottled soda," said Cagney. "Diet."

"Chai will be perfect," said Aidan.

"That will be four Chais and one diet soda, bottled," murmured Yash, hurrying across the lobby, his extra-large shoes squeaking on the polished white floor.

Tess bounded out of her chair and headed towards a glinting display cabinet. Shoving her nose against the glass she let out a low whistle. "Guys. You've got to come see this."

Cagney scowled. "This better not be an exhibition of pink saris through the ages."

"And what would be wrong with that?" asked Tess. "No, come see, this is amazing."

The cousins lumbered out of their comfy seats and crossed the lobby. Gazing into the display case, they were dumbstruck. Glistening on plump, black velvet were diamonds. Huge diamonds.

Tess grinned. "Told you it was good."

"Whoa!" said Lissy. "It says here six of the largest and most famous diamonds in the world are originally from India. The Blue Hope, Orloff, Regent, Mountain of Light, Idols Eye and Sancy all come from various Indian diamond mines."

"Which one's that?" Cagney pointed to a ginormous blue diamond set in a necklace.

"It's a replica of the Blue Hope," said Lissy, following the diagram.

"I want it," said Tess.

"No, you don't," said Lissy. "It says it's put a curse on everyone who's owned it. Marie Antoinette was beheaded after wearing it."

Tess snatched her hands off the cabinet and stuffed them in her pink polka-dot pockets. "Maybe not."

"Legend says the Blue Hope was plucked from the eye of an idol," said Lissy.

"Is there another eye?" asked Aidan.

Lissy read some more. "Says here it's never been found."

"Wow!" said Olivia. "Imagine finding something like that."

"How about that one?" Cagney pointed to a pale yellow sparkle.

"That's a replica of the Sancy," said Lissy. "It was once found inside the stomach of a servant."

"Good grief," said Cagney, grimacing. "That's way too much information."

"You'd need an awful lot of tea to swallow that," said Tess.

Lissy looked up. The distinctive clatter of china could be heard. Instantly, Yash appeared rattling across the lobby. The small boy swayed between the potted plants, holding a tea tray wider than he was. Yash looked up and grinned, but the grin was swiftly wiped off his face when, in one spectacular movement, his feet went in opposite directions.

Slipping on the marble floor, Yash skidded helplessly towards the chairs. Stumbling, he launched the tea tray towards the table. Everyone watched as the tea tray flew silently and, with a weird gracefulness, landed, with a tinkly thud, bang smack in the middle of the tiny table.

Yash lifted his face off the marble, a relieved smile spreading across his sweet face. "Tea," he said, "is served."

15

Uncle Pinky

The cousins slumped into their seats and sipped their drinks.

"So what's the plan?" said Aidan.

Olivia took a large swig of tea and gulped. A sweet gingerbread taste flooded her mouth. Olivia hated gingerbread. She quickly checked to make sure she didn't have an audience before spitting the brown liquid back into the tea cup.

"That good huh?" said Cagney, inhaling a mouthful of soda.

Olivia ignored her. "Well, we've found out where Pinky's staying, now we need to find out his name."

"Yep, I'd forgotten about that," said Aidan.

"But how are we going to find out who he is?" asked Tess.

"That," said Olivia, "is the tricky bit."

"We could ask the desk clerk," said Lissy.

"I don't think they give information about people in hotels like these," said Aidan.

"How do you *know*?" asked Tess. "They might if we ask nicely."

"No," said Cagney. "We need an angle."

"Why don't we pretend we know him?" said Olivia.

"But wouldn't we know his name if we knew him?" said Lissy.

"We could say we forgot," suggested Tess.

Cagney clapped her hands together. "I've got it. We could pretend we're related to him and he's late meeting us."

"Yes," said Aidan. "They're more likely to give us information if we say we're related."

"But we don't look like him," said Lissy.

"*We* don't," said Cagney. "But *they* do."

Cagney, Aidan and Lissy all turned and stared at Olivia and Tess. Cagney's mouth formed a Cheshire cat grin, all teeth and no substance.

"Count me out," said Olivia. "I'm not going to pretend I'm related to a murderer. And stop smiling like that; it's kind of weird."

"But I thought you said it was imperative we find out who he is," said Cagney.

Olivia folded her arms across her tee and hmpfd.

"Don't worry." Tess stood and gave her pink sandals a quick polish on the back of her socks. "I'll take care of it."

Tess approached the mahogany desk and gave the bell a sharp tap. Without delay a man popped up from behind the counter.

"Hello," said the desk clerk. "How may I help you?"

Tess smiled broadly. "Can you tell me if my uncle has returned to his room?"

The desk clerk clicked on his computer. "What is your uncle's name?"

"We call him Uncle Pinky, but that's not his real name."

The desk clerk looked bemused. "I'm glad to hear it. What would be his real name?"

"I don't know," said Tess, her almond eyes starting to mist.

"Little girl, I am very sorry, but I can hardly look up an uncle if you are not knowing his name."

Tess produced a pink flowery hankie and blew her nose loudly. She peered at the desk clerk with brown watery eyes. "*I* don't know," she wailed. "I'm just a kid, how am *I* expected to know these things."

The desk clerk looked distressed. "Well, what does he look like?" He jabbed on the mouse in an effort to raise the computer to life.

Tess lowered her hankie and abruptly stopped crying. "He's five foot six, has black hair, pale skin and he's Chinese."

The desk clerk gawked at her, astounded at the sudden change. "I am sorry, little girl, but I think you just described half of China."

"Also he wears a cream suit and a hat with a bright pink band."

"Oh!" said the desk clerk. "You mean Dr. Fat. He checked in yesterday from Beijing for two nights.

He returned about half an hour ago. Let me tell him his niece is waiting for him."

"No, don't do that," said Tess, quickly. "He's not the most puncturesque of uncles."

The desk clerk frowned. "Are you meaning to say he is not being pretty or not being punctual?"

Tess smiled. "Both! I'll just wait for him in the lobby." Tess turned to go, but swung back. "By the way, what's Uncle Pinky's first name?"

Tess' eyes widened as the desk clerk told her. "No wonder he wants us to call him Uncle Pinky."

Tess turned, and beckoning to the others, headed towards the exit. Clattering their tea cups onto the table, the cousins wrestled themselves out of the armchairs and followed Tess down the steps.

The cousins were in too much of a hurry to notice a figure emerge from behind the potted plants. The man popped a round red candy into his mouth and headed towards the counter. One sharp rap on the bell and, once more, the desk clerk emerged like a jack-in-the-box.

"Aaah! Dr. Fat," he said. "I take it you have found your niece?"

16

The Question of the King

Tess bolted through the door and raced down the steps. The Ambassador purred at the curb as she flung open the door and they all poured in.

Dinkar waited for the door to slam before pulling into traffic. "You found him?"

"Not exactly," said Tess, "but I know who he is."

"Spill," said Olivia.

Tess giggled. "His name is Dr. Dingbang Fat."

The large gulp of soda Cagney had just inhaled, spluttered through the car like mist.

Tess swiped droplets off the ends of her ears and continued. "He flew in yesterday from Beijing for two nights."

"Yeah, right," said Cagney, regaining her composure.

Tess criss-crossed her pointy finger over her pink fuzzy tee. "It's the truth, I'm way too young to come up with a name like that by myself."

"She's got a point," said Olivia.

"I almost feel sorry for him," said Lissy.

Cagney gave her a look.

Lissy shrugged. "Almost."

"Good work, Tess," said Aidan. "But now what do we do?"

Cagney took another impressive slurp of soda. "Go shopping?"

"I think we should tell Miss Gupta," said Lissy. "Maybe she'll know what to do."

"Of course," said Olivia. "Maybe once she hears his name she'll remember who he is."

Settling in her seat, Tess watched the scenery of New Delhi flow by. "Dinkar, is New Delhi really new?"

"That is a very good question, little cousin. In 1911 the British decided to move their capital from Calcutta to Delhi."

"Why on earth would anyone move a capital?" asked Cagney.

Dinkar shrugged. "They were warned not to do it. Legend says he who moves his capital to Delhi will lose it. But the British did it anyway and renamed the city New Delhi."

"Did they lose it?" asked Aidan.

"Look around," said Dinkar. "After being in control for 250 years, the British were overturned and India returned to its people. But actually, the city is not exactly where it should be."

"What do you mean?" asked Tess.

Dinkar grinned. "King George traveled to India to choose the site of his new city, and laid a stone to mark the spot. Two years later the architect arrived, but he did not like this spot."

"But I guess he had no choice," said Aidan.

"You would think," said Dinkar. "But the architect was very determined. Every day he traveled around the area looking for his perfect spot."

"Did he find it?" asked Tess.

"Yes," said Dinkar. "Once the architect had found the spot he liked, he snuck out in the depths of the night with a one-wheeled barrow and moved the stone to this new spot."

"With a wheelbarrow?" asked Olivia.

Dinkar nodded, seriously.

"You're joking, right?" said Cagney.

"I know. It is sounding very ridiculous, even to me."

"Did the king ever find out?" asked Lissy.

"I do not know, little cousin, but here the city is."

"Dinkar, does India have a king?" asked Aidan.

Dinkar leaned hard on the steering wheel emitting the deep resonant horn sound the cousins were getting to know so well. "No, just a parliament and prime minister, like the British."

"What about a queen?" asked Tess.

"We are having no queen either."

"Then if India has no king, who was Pinky talking about?" asked Aidan.

"My mom always says Elvis is the king," said Cagney.

"Who's Elvis?" asked Tess.

Cagney shrugged. "No idea, but he always seems to have left the building."

The Ambassador nudged past government buildings and crawled along wide tree-lined avenues. Finally, seeing a break in the traffic, Dinkar put his foot down and the Ambassador sailed forward.

Just as swiftly as the car gathered speed it started to slow, until it came to a complete stop. At that exact moment the heavens split in two. Tumultuous rain tumbled out of the clouds, rapidly soaking everything and everyone in its path.

"Wow!" said Tess. "I've never seen rain like it. It's like someone's emptying a really big bucket of water."

"It is the monsoon," said Dinkar. "At this time of year it comes every day. But it will go away soon."

"Is that why we've stopped?" asked Lissy.

"No, little cousin, the monsoon is the least of our worries." Dinkar swiveled in his seat to face Cagney, his bony hand outstretched. "Please miss, may I?"

"My soda?" Cagney clutched the bottle to her dress.

"The man's thirsty," said Olivia. "Give Dinkar the drink."

"No, not thirsty," said Dinkar. "Out of petrol, or as you Americans would say, out of gas."

"Oh no!" said Lissy.

"Is there a gas station nearby?" asked Aidan.

"No, we are not being close to any petrol station. It would take very long to walk. But your soda miss, please. May I?"

Cagney reluctantly handed Dinkar the bottle, watched him open the door and step into the drenching rain. Dinkar hurried to the rear of the Ambassador.

Tess scooted around in her seat and peered out the window (which, through the torrents of rain, was harder to do than it sounds). "What's Dinkar doing?"

Olivia rubbed the steaming window with her elbow. "He's unscrewing the gas cap."

"And pouring soda in," said Lissy, in disbelief.

"Apparently it's the car that's thirsty," said Aidan.

Dinkar replaced the cap and hurried back. Flinging open the door he squelched into the driver's seat. Behind the wheel, his drenched body looked like he had swam the Indian Ocean. "Fingers crossed."

Dinkar turned the key and the Ambassador spluttered to life.

"Who'd of thunk it?" said Aidan.

"Not me," said Olivia.

"Once I was with Callie and we had to walk ten miles to the nearest town to get petrol." Dinkar shook the droplets from his dark curly hair. "But your grandma is very good company on such a journey."

"Callie? I mean, Grandma?" asked Aidan.

"Yes, the one and the same. Unfortunately, your Grandma does not drink soda. But I think because of this she has such pretty teeth."

"You know Grandma?" asked Lissy.

"Why of course, little cousin. She and I have long been friends. I was having the great honor of picking her up from the airport just before you."

"So that's where you were," said Tess.

"Where did you take her?" asked Olivia.

"Aah, little cousin, that is a secret I cannot be telling."

"Why not?" asked Cagney.

Dinkar smiled his large, toothless grin. "I am only the get-away driver, remember?"

Ten minutes later, Dinkar swerved the Ambassador onto the steaming sidewalk and bounced to a stop outside a pretty cottage. A well-tended winding path led to the whimsical abode, with smoke rising from its crooked chimney, tiny glass panes dotting the windows and a welcoming red door. It reminded Aidan of something, but he couldn't remember what.

The rain had now passed and the air clung hot and sticky as the cousins crawled out of the Ambassador and took in the view.

"This is where you will be staying," said Dinkar, proudly.

Tess squealed with delight. "It's perfect. It's fabulous. It's just like Hansel and Gretel," she said, before skipping up the garden path and disappearing through the front door.

17

The Curry House

The inside of Miss Gupta's house did not look like the outside. To say it was messy was an understatement of humongous proportions. In fact, Olivia could only think of one place worse. Unfortunately that place belonged to her sister.

The cousins inched into a disheveled living room and picked their way across the crowded floor. On the walls clung pictures of tigers. Small tigers, huge tigers, furry tigers and happy tigers. Miss Gupta featured in several of these pictures. Her face carried an easy smile and a tenderness, that was seriously lacking when dealing with the cousins.

Aidan ran a finger across the stacks of books littering the floor, his face alight with pleasure. "She sure likes to read."

"Ya think?" said Olivia, tripping over a huge book entitled *India's Man Eaters*.

Miss Gupta stood in the doorway wearing a green flowery apron, licking a long ladle. "I've made a traditional North Indian dish. I hope you like tandoori?"

Everyone turned towards Cagney.

Cagney smiled sweetly and crossed her fingers behind her back. "My favorite!"

The cousins emerged from the kitchen with bowls of rice and a dollop of bright orange chicken. Shifting books off an odd assortment of chairs, they began to eat.

"So?" said Miss Gupta, letting out a humongous burp that even Olivia would have been proud of. "Tell me everything."

Olivia told Miss Gupta about the market. Cagney told her about the bus ride and Aidan told her about the elephant. Finally they got to the part about the hotel and Miss Gupta sat up and put down her bowl.

"His name is Dr. Dingbang Fat," said Tess, a blob of sauce perched on the end of her button nose.

"He's from Beijing and he's staying at the British Grenadier. But tomorrow he is going to Agra."

"You have done well," said Miss Gupta. "You cousins are everything your grandma said you were and more."

"Really?" asked Tess, happy at the unexpected compliment.

"Really," said Miss Gupta.

"Do you recognize the name?" asked Aidan.

"It is familiar," said Miss Gupta, frowning. "Very familiar, but I can't quite remember. Maybe a night's rest will jog my brain."

Lissy coughed shyly and glanced towards Miss Gupta. "Do *you* know our grandma?"

"She is a great friend of my father," said Miss Gupta, grasping a framed picture of a baby tiger and a much younger Grandma. "I remember her from when I was a little girl. She used to help me with my tigers. This one is Sashi. She was a particular favorite of both mine and your grandma's."

"Grandma Callie helped you with tigers?" asked Lissy, grasping the frame and staring into Grandma Callie's piercing blue eyes.

"Yes," said Miss Gupta. "The woman has absolutely no fear."

Aidan and Olivia glanced at each other in amazement. Was there anything about their grandma that wouldn't surprise them? Up until two days ago, they had no idea their grandma had even been to India, not to mention hanging out with tigers.

"But it is interesting," said Miss Gupta.

"What's interesting?" asked Aidan, passing the frame to Olivia.

"That Dr. Fat is going to Agra."

"Why is it interesting?" asked Cagney.

"Because that is where *you* are going tomorrow. Dinkar will take you to the train station in the early morning."

"You're not coming with us?" asked Lissy.

"Not straight away. I have a few things I need to finish at the zoo. I will bring your bags and meet you at the Agra train station in the evening."

"Are we going to see Grandma?" asked Lissy.

"I am not sure if she's found her–"

"Found what?" asked Olivia, quickly.

Miss Gupta's eyes clouded and her mouth tightened as a look of extreme sadness passed over her pretty face.

Aidan sighed. "Nobody ever tells us anything."

Miss Gupta blinked and swiped her eyes with the back of her hand. "Just keep an eye on our Dr. Fat and soon, hopefully, I will remember where I have heard his name."

Tess emerged from licking the bottom of her bowl, a circular orange stain ringing her forehead. "But what is Agra?"

Miss Gupta rose and strode into the kitchen. "You'll soon find out."

The girls did not sleep well. After being thrown cushions and a few silk blankets, Miss Gupta turned off the light and told them not to damage her books.

"How come Aidan gets the spare room?" whispered Cagney.

Tess repeated the words Miss Gupta had said earlier. "Coz it's tiny and we wouldn't all fit."

"Don't blind me with logic," said Cagney, nose to page with a rather smelly book on pythons.

Tess' head emerged from beneath blue silk, a flashlight in one hand, a glossy magazine in the other.

"Tess, what are you doing under there?" Lissy struggled up and flipped on the light.

"This is fascinating," said Tess. "Did you know India has a film industry bigger than Hollywood, and you'll never guess what it's called. No, don't even bother. It's called Bollywood," she said, with a squeal.

Tess had dreams of being in the movies. People told her all the time she looked like a Chinese Snow White. Tess figured if they ever made a remake, she would definitely get the part.

"I don't believe it." Olivia grabbed the magazine and flipped the page. She read aloud. "Indian films last three to four hours and are watched by over eleven million people."

"That's not so many," said Cagney.

"Eleven million every day," finished Olivia.

"No way." Cagney reached for the magazine and tugged it out of Olivia's hands. "It says India has more millionaires than the U.S. and wow, look at that sari."

A noise in the hallway made the girls freeze.

"Quick," said Cagney. "It's Miss Gupta."

Lissy sprung up, hit the light and the girls dove under their blankets. By the time Miss Gupta had stomped her way to the door, all she could hear were the gentle, if somewhat fake, snores of four sleepy children.

∗
✳ ✳
∗

18

The Tomb

inkar skidded towards the train station, scattering passengers like confetti as he barreled onto the curb. "Before I forget," he said, handing an envelope to Cagney, "Miss Gupta was leaving this for you before she left for the zoo this morning."

Cagney stuffed the envelope into her day-pack.

"Goodbye, little cousins."

Tess simultaneously gave his bones a crushing hug and let out a humongous sneeze. "Oops! Sorry Dinkar," she said, brushing bits off his shirt.

Dinkar smiled broadly. "Enjoy Agra!" he shouted, before slumping into the driver's seat and disappearing into the crowd.

The cousins worked their way into the station and studied the large information board.

"There," said Cagney. "The 7:10am train to Agra. Platform Two."

The cousins wound their way through the crowds of people until they found what they were looking for. Leaning against a sign asking them not to spit, they surveyed the chaos.

People were everywhere. Sitting, standing, lying; you name it, they were doing it. It also seemed that an acceptable way of getting from platform to platform was across the tracks. Lissy had not spent a lot of time on trains back home, but she was pretty sure this was not the way Amtrak worked.

Olivia watched a scruffy puppy dog sniff her way across the steel rails. "I hope that dog's not going to get hit."

Cagney edged away from a couple of children who were reaching towards her camera. "I wouldn't worry," she said, opening the wrapper on a Twinkie bar. "Unlike us, I'm sure she's totally used to it, scrawny little mutt."

It was unclear whether the scrawny little mutt saw the wrapper, smelled the wrapper or heard the wrapper. But no sooner had Cagney finished speaking than the little dog's head tilted to the left and, in one spectacular leap, she bounded onto the platform heading straight for Cagney.

Cagney saw the blur of fur streaking towards her and stumbled backwards, her hands flapping in an effort to discourage. "Ugh! Get away from me, you mangy ... flea-ridden–"

But it was no good; the dog was lolloping in her direction. Cagney dropped to her knees, covered her frizzy locks and prayed the dog didn't have rabies. For one incredible moment it looked like the dog would leapfrog right over Cagney's head. But at the last minute, she skidded to a stop, lifted her head and gave Cagney's face a good solid lick. A second later, she tore down the platform, a Twinkie in her mouth, her waggy tail swishing behind her.

Tess slapped a pink flowery handkerchief into Cagney's hand and pulled her cousin to her feet. "I'm thinking we just forget that ever happened."

Cagney wiped the drool from her ears and spun around. "Come back here you scrawny mutt. I'm going to …"

But the cousins were unable to hear what Cagney would do, as her words became buried beneath a deafening HEEERE HAAWE, and a second later a thundering train stormed through the station. The train careened along the track. Women clutched their saris, men held down their billowing pajamas and Lissy and Tess clasped each other as their hair flew high into the jet stream.

"Whoa!" Aidan felt his teeth. "I think that train dislodged a filling."

Olivia searched the platform for the puppy dog. "I hope she wasn't on the track when that train went by. She'd be squashed flatter than a tortilla."

The train to Agra already bulged with people, and the cousins jostled their way along the aisle until they miraculously found seats. Tess slipped in next to the window and the others piled around her.

Cagney scrutinized the bars covering windows, which were sorely in need of a wash. "I feel like I'm in prison."

"I feel like I could eat," said Tess, blowing her nose.

Immediately, wiry hands plunged through the metal bars, grabbing Tess' stripy pink tee-shirt.

"Chai, miss?"

"Chapati?"

"Kaffe?" came voices from the other side of the bars.

Tess tried unsuccessfully to move away. "Yikes! I'm not that hungry."

Olivia wrestled the grasping hands off her sister, but as soon as one released, another seized.

"Thank you, but we don't want any chickens," said Lissy, trying to reason with the increasing vendors.

"Or goats," added Tess.

"Or porcupines," said Aidan, eyeing a very prickly specimen of Lord only knew what.

Within seconds, bony fingers grabbed Lissy's dress and she, too, was pulled toward the open window.

Cagney tried to remove the hand grasping Lissy's wrist. "This is ridiculous. I thought you said these people understood English?"

"They're not listening," said Olivia, unsuccessfully trying to detangle the many hands that had a firm hold on all parts of Tess' tee-shirt.

"How do you stop them?" cried Cagney.

Tess wrestled her hands free and, smacking them together, closed her eyes and began mumbling.

Olivia peered dumbfounded at her sister. "It's official," she said, shaking her head. "She's finally lost it."

"Tess, are you okay?" asked Aidan.

Tess opened one eye. "I'm praying to Ganesha."

"Who?" asked Olivia.

"The elephant god," said Lissy. "The one who makes projects go smoothly."

"Exactly," said Tess.

"Good grief," said Cagney. "Do you really think a fat elephant …" Cagney stopped as all the hands disappeared through the bars.

"Whoa!" said Aidan.

Tess opened both eyes and smiled. Instantly the train lurched forward. Tess looked crestfallen. "Ah, fooey!"

"Hey," said Aidan. "Who's to say it wasn't Ganesha."

"Just be careful who you tell you're hungry," said Olivia, settling into her seat.

The train gathered speed. Cagney peered at the view, squinting to see more clearly through the grimy window. Removing her glasses, she cleaned them with the bottom of Tess' tee. She could have sworn there were bunches of people squatting on the sides of the tracks.

"I can't believe people are sitting so close to the trains," said Olivia.

Lissy leaned forward. "What are they doing?"

Aidan grinned. "I don't think you want to know."

The girls peered out the window and recoiled with horror. Olivia began laughing, Cagney reached for a packet of scented tissues, and Lissy gaped, open-mouthed.

"Hey guys!" said Tess. "I think they're going to the bathroom!"

Urban New Delhi was soon replaced by fields of green, dotted with fluttering saris drying, like splashes of poppies, in the breeze.

"So what exactly is Agra?" asked Olivia, as Lissy pulled Spider from her duffle bag.

Lissy gave Spider a few clicks, leaned back and smiled. "Of course, I should have remembered." Spinning Spider around so the others could see, she began to read. "The Taj Mahal was a tomb built in Agra by Shah Jahan as a memorial to his favorite wife, Mumtaz Mahal."

"What's a tomb?" asked Tess.

"It's a place where people are buried," said Aidan.

"And what do you mean 'favorite' wife?" asked Cagney.

"His religion allowed more than one," answered Lissy.

"Whoa," said Olivia. "That's intense."

"The Taj Mahal was built over 350 years ago. One thousand elephants brought marble blocks from 200 miles away. It took 20,000 men twenty years to complete," Lissy continued.

"Yikes!" said Olivia. "That's an awful long time to build a headstone."

"Why did it take so long?" asked Tess, sniffling.

"You try building anything in this heat," said Aidan. "I guess they had to take a lot of breaks. Drink a lot of tea."

Lissy scrolled down and clicked on a small pale picture. The Taj Mahal popped onto Spider's screen and the cousins took a collective breath.

"Wow!" said Tess.

"Yeah, that would take a few years to put together," said Olivia.

On the screen gleamed the most beautiful building Aidan had ever seen. A delicate white structure with an impressive dome rose into an azure sky, while four tall pillars resembling skinny lighthouses, stiff like soldiers, stood guard. In front of the building lay a long strip of water that reflected the shrine perfectly.

"That's the biggest headstone I ever saw," said Tess.

"How many have you seen?" asked Olivia.

"Not that many. But I'm pretty sure that's the biggest."

"That's not a tomb," said Cagney. "That's a palace."

"It was built to prove his love to Mumtaz. In fact, it's really unusual, as most tombs in India are built for men," said Lissy.

"Way to go, Mumtaz," said Olivia.

"Is she the only one buried there?" asked Aidan.

"No, her husband is too."

"Aah, that's sweet." Tess stifled another snuffle.

Olivia edged away from her sister. "Don't give it to me."

Tess blew her nose "Give you what?"

"Your cold, Doofus."

"What cold?" said Tess.

Olivia rolled her eyes. "How can anybody catch a cold in hundred-degree weather?"

Tess looked up. Her button nose a delicate shade of cherry. "Just lucky I guess."

Lissy smiled at the sisters and continued reading. "Spider says, soon after Shah Jahan built the mausoleum, he lost his kingdom to his son who imprisoned him in a nearby fort."

"Oh, that's sad." Tess wiggled her nose in a valiant effort not to sneeze.

"The poor man got to spend the rest of his life looking out his cell at what he had created," said Lissy.

Cagney surveyed the bars on the train windows and sighed. "I'm beginning to know exactly how he felt."

$*$ $*$ $*$

19

Taj Mahal

The cousins were greeted in Agra the same way they left New Delhi. Cagney and Lissy glanced away, but much to Aidan's amusement, Tess waved, although everyone seemed to be a little too occupied to wave back.

After several hot, crowded hours, all five were anxious to stretch their legs. As soon as the train stopped, the cousins grabbed their day-packs, leapt onto the platform and exited the station.

Olivia noticed an Ambassador pass by. "Taxi!" she yelled.

"No, we need to take one of those." Lissy pointed across the road at a horse and buggy.

"Great!" said Tess. "But why?"

"Well, for one because they look kind of fun and two, because Spider says no vehicles are permitted around the Taj Mahal."

"Why on earth not?" asked Cagney.

"To protect it from pollution," replied Lissy. "The Taj Mahal is a World Heritage site, I'm assuming they'd like it to stay a sight for as long as possible."

Cagney approached the buggy and jumped aboard. The others scrambled up behind her. "The Taj Mahal, please."

The driver cupped his ear.

"I think he's deaf," said Aidan, wishing he'd thought to bring scented tissues of his own.

"I said the TAJ MAHAL," bellowed Cagney.

The buggy man nodded, flipped the reins and the scrawny horse pulled into a narrow congested street.

The roads of Agra made those of New Delhi seem tame. Within seconds the horse-and-buggy was fighting for space, zig-zagging down the bumpy road in an un-choreographed dance. With several hundred rickshaws, a dozen cycles and one or two water buffaloes bumping alongside, the chaos was truly spectacular.

Aidan considered the buggy, which was doorless, seatbeltless and would never pass any standardized testing in the U.S. Consisting of one long bench and a small covered roof, it was plenty spacious enough for one or even two, but with five it was a bit of a squish. A small motorbike transporting its wiry driver, his pregnant wife, a baby, a basket of rice, two small children, a goat and three geese passed them on the left. Aidan reassessed his opinion of the buggy, in comparison it was practically palatial.

Twenty minutes later, the horse slowed to a trot. Other than breaking twice for errant cows and almost losing Tess on a particularly sharp bend, the journey had been uneventful.

"The entryway," explained Lissy, leaning forward to pay the driver.

The cousins tumbled out of the buggy and headed towards a squat square building. After purchasing tickets and passing through security, the five rounded a corner and came to a stop. In the distance, the delicate white façade rose majestically into a pale blue sky. Moving to the end of the long rectangular pond, the five gazed at the perfectly symmetrical structure and its gently rippling reflection.

Cagney snatched up her camera and began snapping.

Lissy led everyone towards the mausoleum. "These gardens were quite different when it was first built in 1648. But they fell into disrepair."

"That's so sad," said Tess, blowing her nose. "I hate to think of flowers all dried and wilty."

"When the British arrived they re-created the gardens and changed them to look like the gardens in England."

"So the British weren't so bad after all," said Aidan.

"What are the lighthouses for?" Olivia pointed at the four towers surrounding the tomb. "Are we near the sea?"

"They're minarets," said Lissy.

Tess leapt in front of the minaret that Cagney focused on and struck a pose. Cagney rolled her eyes and snapped the picture.

Tess curtsied. "What's a minaret?"

"It's a tower attached to a mosque that calls people to prayer," said Lissy.

"Oh," said Tess, "they sure are pretty."

"Have you noticed that everything is completely symmetrical?" asked Lissy. "Everything is balanced."

Olivia observed the bushes reflected in pairs either side of the pool. She didn't really care for gardening and the smell of flowers was bringing on her allergies. Still, even she had to admit it was beautiful, in a girlish kind of 'fufu' way.

"They call the large dome the onion," said Lissy, admiring the towering marble walls.

"Hope it doesn't smell," said Tess.

Olivia snorted.

"What?" said Tess. "Onions make me cry."

Cagney passed Tess a tissue. "You're so snuffly, you wouldn't be able to smell it even if it was a giant onion."

"Talking of all things stinky, has anyone seen Pinky yet?" asked Olivia.

"What with trying not to lose Tess out the buggy and seeing the Taj Mahal, I quite forgot about him," said Aidan.

"Never mind," said Olivia. "I'm sure he'll turn up sooner than later."

The cousins ascended the marble steps.

"It's a shoe sale," said Tess, pointing towards a jumble of shoes laying higgledy-piggledy to their right.

"You have to go bare foot," said Lissy, unbuckling her sandals and placing them near the pile.

The others followed her lead. Aidan was glad it was still early. Right now the marble felt cool and slick under his feet, a few hours from now he had a feeling it wouldn't be so cool.

The inside of the Taj Mahal was as beautiful as the outside. Precious jewels inlaid into the marble made the vision as delicate as it was intricate.

"The stones come from all over Asia," said Lissy. "Crystal and jade from China, turquoise from Tibet and sapphires from Sri Lanka."

Cagney inspected the colorful stones and tried to imagine a large lump of jade nestling in a necklace around her neck. She smiled. "Now *that's* interesting."

The effect was truly breathtaking. The cousins entered a pale octagonal room with two elaborately decorated coffins in the middle. Cagney put a scented tissue to her nose and looked away.

"They're not the real coffins," explained Lissy.

"What do you mean?" asked Olivia.

"The real ones are in a vault underneath. These are fake."

"Oh good," said Cagney, removing the tissue.

"Muslim tradition forbids graves being elaborately decorated. Mumtaz and Shah Jahan are actually in a plain crypt beneath us. Spider said their faces are turned to the right."

"Why the right?" asked Aidan.

"Because that's the way to Mecca."

"What's Mecca?" asked Tess, grabbing another tissue and stifling yet another sneeze.

"It's the holiest place in the world for Muslims, and Mumtaz and Shah Jahan were Muslim," said Lissy.

Tess cocked her head to one side and studied the two coffins. "Do you notice anything weird about those coffins?"

"Yep," said Aidan. The two coffins were similar, but one had a larger base and was even more elaborate. "They're the only thing in this entire mausoleum that's not symmetrical."

"The bigger one is Shah Jahan's," said Lissy.

"Figures," said Olivia.

A sudden trill made Olivia look up. Through the tourists she could just make out someone in the corner struggling to silence a cell phone. As the owner of the cell phone beat a hasty retreat, Olivia was treated to a flash of scarlet, and the tip of a cream-colored hat.

20

A Narrow Escape

Olivia watched Pinky push through the tourists and head into the heat. Olivia locked eyes with Aidan. He had seen him too.

"Quick, you get the others and I'll follow him," she whispered.

Pinky emerged into the daylight, his cell phone clasped to his ear, and headed towards a sliver of shade by a towering minaret. Aidan rounded up the girls and together they trailed quietly behind him. As Pinky disappeared behind the minaret, the cousins tiptoed towards the tower and squeezed behind it. Olivia could no longer see Pinky, but she could most definitely hear him.

"Idiots," he hissed. "Can you not do anything right ... I am on the 7:30 train to Gerta. I will be with you by eight o'clock tomorrow. I will deal with you then, and," he said, lowering his voice to barely a squeak, "keep him alive until I get there."

Pinky's footsteps could be heard coming towards them. Just in time, the five slipped around the minaret as Pinky came into view and strode across the mausoleum's grounds.

"Aaaacho!" sneezed Tess.

Pinky stopped and slowly turned.

"Quick!" Olivia crammed everyone behind the narrow structure. But it was too late. Looking around Olivia realized they were trapped. There was nowhere else to go. Footsteps could be heard hurrying across the marble – footsteps getting closer.

"Excuse me!" came a stern voice.

Olivia's heart missed a beat.

Cagney turned and glared at Tess, but the sight was so comical not even Cagney could fail to see the funny side. Tess stood straw straight. To her right was Aidan, his finger wedged under her nose. To her left, Lissy, shoving a pink flowery hankie against Tess' open mouth.

"I said, excuse me," the stern voice repeated.

"Who me?" replied Pinky.

"Day bags are not allowed at the Taj Mahal."

"Hmm?" Pinky inched farther towards the minaret.

"I am afraid you are going to have to come with me."

Olivia looked at Aidan in disbelief.

"But I simply need to ..."

"I am very sorry, but there are no exceptions," said the stern voice.

"But I dropped something behind the minaret," squeaked Pinky. "If I might just–"

Olivia heard another couple of steps head in their direction.

"No Sir, I am needing you to come with me. Once we are storing your day bag you can return and search for whatever it is you are misplacing."

Olivia heard two sets of footsteps retreat into the distance and peeked around the side of the minaret just in time to see Pinky turn and give her a vicious stare.

"Whoa," said Olivia, retreating into the shade.

Tess let out an almighty sneeze.

"Gesundheit," said the four together.

"You're welcome," said Tess.

"I have a bad feeling about this," said Aidan.

"I think we all do," said Lissy.

"Do you think he saw us?" asked Tess.

Cagney's eyebrows disappeared beneath her curls.

Tess took her pink flowery hankie from Lissy and blew her ruddy nose. "I'll take that as a yes."

"Well, at least he's out of the way for a while," said Olivia. "It's going to take him at least an hour to reach the front gate, check his bag and get back through security."

"Hopefully we'll be able to avoid him for the rest of the day," said Aidan.

"Yeah," said Tess. "This place is huge. I'd bet my pink dangly bangles we're never going to see him again."

"Want to bet?" said Cagney.

The cousins spent the rest of the day wandering through the ornate buildings and gardens. Sitting on a bench, at the foot of the long reflecting pool, they rubbed their tired feet and gazed at the graceful beauty of Mumtaz's tomb.

"Well hello," said a high-pitched voice.

The cousins scooted around and there, behind them, stood Pinky.

Cagney turned to face Tess and, motioning towards Tess' bangles, held out her hand.

"Ah fooey!" Tess slipped off her bracelets and handed them to Cagney.

Pinky unwrapped another candy and let the wrapper drift to the floor. "I think we need to have a little chat. You know," he crunched down hard, "friend to friend."

Lissy eyed Pinky with undisguised dislike, as she added litterbug to Pinky's list of unattractive qualities.

"I don't mean to be rude," said Olivia. "But we're not your friends."

"But I thought I was your Uncle Pinky, no?"

Tess gasped.

"You should be careful what you say in deserted lobbies," said Pinky. "It can be heard by the wrong kind of people."

"You don't scare us," said Olivia.

"Why should you be scared of me?" asked Pinky.

"Because we know all about your plan to murder the king." Tess slapped a hand over her mouth, her eyes wide like dinner plates, but it was too late.

Pinky's face looked thunderous. "You know nothing," he hissed, drawing closer to Tess.

Aidan bounded forward and moved Tess behind him.

Pinky drew nearer and unable to reach Tess, wrapped a clammy hand around Aidan's throat. "Stay out of my business," he squeaked. "You do not want to get involved. I am *way* out of your league."

Aidan gasped for air. He was turning rather red and his knees weren't feeling too good either.

"Let him go," said Tess, dissolving into sneezes.

"You're hurting him," said Olivia, scrambling to her feet.

"I will say this once, and only once. If I ever see you children again, it will be more than his neck I hurt."

"You're a big bully," said Lissy, and rushing at Pinky, she pushed him clean into the reflecting pond.

21

Identity of the King

The cousins tore out of the Taj Mahal and did not stop. Terrified of coming face to face with Pinky and unable to get a ride, they raced all the way to the station and they were late. Very late. The cousins barreled down the platform, clutching their sides, panting with exhaustion.

"There you are." Miss Gupta ushered them onto the train seconds before it lurched forward along the track.

The cousins followed her to a compartment. Throwing open the door, they saw six beds stacked three high, their backpacks thrown in a heap on the floor. The five piled into the room, threw themselves onto the bunks and started talking.

"For the love of pizza," said Miss Gupta, raising a hand. "One at a time."

Cagney briefly explained what had happened at the Taj Mahal. Miss Gupta went from brown, to white to thunder.

Standing, she pounded the bunk bed with her fist. "Does nobody in this family have an inch of intelligence?"

"I'm intelligent," said Tess, twirling her pigtails.

"Did none of you nincompoops read the note I left you this morning?"

Tess looked blanker still.

"Oh, the note!" Cagney reached into her day-pack.

Scrunched in the front pocket she pulled out a forlorn looking envelope, tore it open and read aloud.

"I have remembered who he is
Under NO circumstances approach this man.
He is highly dangerous."

"Oops!" said Lissy.

"Who is he?" asked Olivia.

"He is a wicked man," said Miss Gupta. "An evil, treacherous murderer."

Tess gulped.

"Who has he murdered?" asked Cagney.

"Tigers," said Miss Gupta, a lone tear travelling to her nose. "Hundreds of tigers."

Lissy plucked an apple-scented tissue from Cagney's hand and passed it to Miss Gupta. "Can you bear to talk about it?"

Miss Gupta ignored the tissue, nodded and wiped her nose on the back of her arm. "When he first came to the zoo, I knew I'd seen him before. But the name Dr. Dingbang Fat. It was the doctor that threw me, not to mention the Dingbang. He's no more a doctor than I am."

"Then what is he?" asked Tess.

"He's an herbalist, steeped in the ancient, mumbo jumbo of Chinese medicine."

"But what does an herbalist have to do with killing tigers?" asked Olivia.

"They sell the body parts for medicine," said Miss Gupta.

"Medicine?" said Lissy, confused. "What does a tiger have to do with medicine?"

Miss Gupta sighed deeply. "Some people believe tigers have great medicinal purposes."

"Why?" asked Aidan.

"Some think tiger bones cure rheumatism, that tiger tails cure skin disease and tiger whiskers give you courage. A single tiger paw is worth as much as $1,000."

"That's horrible," said Olivia.

Miss Gupta nodded. "People have been raised to think that the paw of a tiger will stop evil spirits from entering your home."

Lissy shook her head in disbelief. "Who in their right mind believes this?"

"Many people in China," said Miss Gupta.

"That's ridiculous," said Aidan. "Isn't it?"

"Yes. But it is hard to change what people think, and harder still to break traditions that have been the same for thousands of years."

"Of course," Aidan rummaged through his day-pack. "That's what the shop in the market was. I transcribed it last night with my *Scribbling Sanskrit* book. We've been so busy I forgot to tell anyone."

Aidan found the grubby notebook, pulled it out and read,

"Chinese Herbal Medicine
Dr. Huang Fu Lu."

"But we overheard Pinky saying he was going to kill the king," said Olivia. "Nothing was said about tigers."

Miss Gupta slapped herself on the forehead. "I was blind. Tigers *are* the kings. The kings of the jungle."

"A Whim away a whim away" mumbled Tess, wiggling her hips as she launched into an extremely off-key rendition of *The Lion Sleeps Tonight.*

Cagney slapped a palm in front of her cousin's mouth. Tess stepped backwards. "But I thought *lions* were the kings of the jungle?"

"In Africa, yes, but in India, it is the tiger who is king."

"Well, it's too late now," said Cagney. "He's on the 7:30 train to Gerta."

Miss Gupta stood so violently, she smacked her head on the bunk above.

"Don't tell me," said Lissy. "This *is* the 7:30 train to Gerta."

22

Trapped

Miss Gupta flipped open her cell phone and let out a strangled cry. "Okay, I'm going to see if I can get some reception on this train. I've got to let my father know." Entering the passageway she let the door slam behind her.

Olivia unlatched the door and watched Miss Gupta head along the corridor. "Come on. I'm starving. Let's find some food."

"Where are we going to get food from?" asked Lissy.

"Can't you feel it?" said Olivia. "The train is slowing. That means we're coming into a station, and what do we find at stations?"

Tess' beaming face peeked through the top of her luminous pink poncho. "Did somebody say food?"

"All we have to do is find an open window, and it'll be like the drive-through at Whataburger," said Olivia, her dimple deepening.

"Ooh, I *like* Whataburger," said Tess.

"I tell you, we should stay here and wait," said Cagney.

"I didn't hear Miss Gupta say that," said Olivia. "Did anyone hear Miss Gupta say that?"

"All I heard was the door slamming," said Aidan, whose stomach rumbled as he joined Olivia in the corridor.

"She's going to be mad," said Lissy.

"She's always mad," said Aidan.

"Aah, she won't even know we're gone," said Olivia. "I'd say we have a good twenty minutes. But to be safe, let's go this way." Olivia pointed in the opposite direction to which Miss Gupta had headed.

"Very wise," said Aidan.

"But what if we run into Pinky?" asked Lissy.

"Details!" said Olivia. "When did you become so detail-oriented?"

"I've always been detail-oriented," said Lissy, looking confused.

"Oh yeah!" said Olivia. "I knew it was one of us."

"Besides, what are the chances on a huge train like this?" said Aidan.

Cagney raised her arm and rattled Tess' bangles. Reluctantly she followed the others into the corridor. "We're going to regret this."

Whereas Miss Gupta had headed towards the front of the train, the cousins headed towards the rear. The train was busy, but not as packed as the one from New Delhi. Soon they began to enjoy hopping from carriage to carriage in search of empty seats and, just as the train pulled into the station, they finally found an unoccupied window spot.

"Say the magic words," said Olivia.

Tess threw up her arms dramatically. "I'm hungry!"

"And let there be food," said Olivia, with a flourish.

Immediately, arms came clamoring through the open bars.

Twenty minutes later, the cousins had eaten their fill of rice, curries and various assorted Indian food in bright-colored foil.

Cagney scrunched the remaining foil into a ball and aimed it at Aidan's head. "That was good. Maybe Indian food isn't as bad as I thought."

"Come on," said Olivia. "Let's get to the carriage before Miss Gupta finds we're missing."

"Yeah," said Tess. "I could do without coming face to toe with a murderer twice in one day."

"Don't worry," said Aidan, hoisting Tess to her feet. "Unless you paint yourself black and orange I think you're safe."

Tess was half-way down the carriage when the door flung open and in sidled a very damp, very disheveled, Chinese man. In one synchronized move, the five turned and dove for cover. Aiming for the gap between the backs of the seats, they landed in a tangled heap on the floor.

Cagney shifted sideways in an attempt to remove Aidan's elbow from her ear and patted the ground for her glasses. "Okay, 'Miss I'm Starving', what are we going to do now?"

"To be honest, we really should have thought this through more," said Lissy, who lay squashed at the bottom of the pile.

"You're the detail person," said Olivia. "I blame you."

Lissy gave her cousin a kick.

"Hey, that's me," said Tess, who was bent double, her bottom squished against the back of a chair.

Lissy gave Tess an apologetic smile, although it was hugely doubtful Tess saw it, and kicked again.

"You've got to stop kicking," said Aidan, rubbing his shin, which was located somewhere above his neck. "Can anyone see if he's heading this way?"

"Do you want the good news or the bad?" asked Olivia, who had landed at the top of the pile and had the only decent view.

"The good," said Lissy. "In the name of Great Aunt Maud, tell me the good."

"He's sitting a couple of seats ahead of us," said Olivia.

"And the bad?" asked Aidan.

"He's facing this way."

"Great," said Cagney. "Just great."

"What are we going to do?" said Tess, who was starting to get an itch.

"Well, whatever you do, don't sneeze," said Olivia.

Tess squinted at her sister cross-eyed. "I *wasn't* going to. But now you've gone and mentioned it ..."

Cagney looked at Tess' contorted face. "What are you doing?"

"Trying not to sneeze," said Tess, wriggling her nose desperately.

"Well, we can't stay here all night," said Lissy.

"What do you suggest we do?" asked Cagney.

"We're going to need to create a diversion," said Lissy.

"Excellent idea," said Olivia. "How?"

"No idea," said Lissy.

"We could try the elephant god again," said Tess.

Instantly the lights went off and the compartment pitched into black.

"This is getting way spooky," said Cagney.

"Good enough for me." Olivia toppled into the aisle. One by one, the cousins untangled themselves and felt their way to their feet.

"Quick!" said Lissy. "Let's get out of here."

The cousins groped their way down the aisle and would have almost made it if it hadn't been for three things: a sneeze, light and extremely bad luck.

"Achoo," said Tess.

"Bless you," said a squeaky voice, which was at once illuminated by the overhead lights springing back to life.

Tess briefly saw the recognition on Pinky's face. Hastily, he tottered to his feet blocking their exit. Seconds later they were once again plunged into darkness.

Olivia tore back along the aisle. "This way!" she cried.

Olivia flung open the door and tumbled outside. One by one the cousins shot threw the opening onto a rickety metal ledge and slammed the door behind them. In the dark it was hard to see, but one thing was immediately apparent. The cousins realized they had reached the end of the train. There was nowhere else to go.

23

Escape

The cousins clung to the back of the caboose as the train hurtled along. The ledge was not wide and it was not safe. A low metal guard rail was all that kept them from plummeting onto the tracks below. Clinging to a scrawny ladder, Cagney wondered if this could possibly be the worst day of her life. She couldn't be sure, but was pretty certain this featured heavily in the top five.

Olivia surveyed their options. There were few to choose from. The train was traveling way too fast to jump, and in front of them lay nothing but track. Suddenly the train faltered. Clutching the ladder, Olivia instantly heard the screech of brakes. Peering around the side of the train she let out a sigh of relief. "We're coming to another station."

"Great," said Aidan. "Soon as the train stops, let's bail from this death trap and get back to our carriage, pronto. I don't care if we starve to death. No one is going back out."

The approaching lights seemed to take forever, but eventually they were there, and the train squealed to a halt.

"Quick," yelled Aidan, bundling Lissy onto the platform.

Lissy took two steps and stopped dead. "No, wait. Go back!"

"What's wrong now?" asked Cagney, hovering halfway down the steps.

Lissy pushed Cagney back onto the caboose and scrambled up behind her. "He's on the platform. He's heading this way."

"Not a problem." Aidan grabbed the door handle and gave it a sharp twist. "We'll go through the carriage instead."

Aidan wrenched the handle to the left, he slammed it to the right. The door wasn't budging.

"Here, let me." Cagney batted Aidan out the way, grabbed the handle and gave it an almighty tug.

Finally the handle gave way, sheering off in her hand. Dumbstruck, she held it up. "Don't blame me. *He's* the one who loosened it."

Lissy snatched the handle and tossed it onto the track. "This is not good."

"What about this way," said Tess, following the discarded handle.

"No!" Olivia grabbed her sister by the hood of her pink poncho and hoisted her back onto the train. "Do you remember how fast trains can travel through stations?"

Tess rearranged her poncho. "Then where?"

Olivia looked at Cagney and shrugged. "You're not going to like this. You're not going to like this *one* bit."

Scooting up the ladder, Aidan peered down at his sister's pale face and threw out his hand. "Come on, Cagney, you can do it."

Cagney shook her head. "No way."

"You have to." Olivia grabbed her cousin and pushed her towards the ladder. Shoving her skyward, Olivia did not ease up until Cagney disappeared onto the roof. Quickly the others followed. Panting, they lay flat on the top of the train, not daring to breath as they heard Pinky climb onto the caboose.

Tess' nose began to twitch. Taking tiny sniffs she tried desperately to stifle the snuffle heading down her nose. It was no good. Burying her head into her poncho, Tess let out an almighty sneeze.

"Heeeehawww!" Tess frowned at the sound that came from her nose. For a second she wondered if her cold was something deadly. Seconds later Tess realized it wasn't her sneeze at all. It was the express train about to whiz by on the track next door. The track where seconds before she had stood.

"Hang on," yelled Aidan, as the impact bombarded the stationary train, rattling it to its core. The cousins gripped the roof with all their might, knowing certain death awaited if they fell.

After what seemed like an eternity, the train stopped rocking. Olivia looked up to see the express train streaking into the distance.

Tess glanced down onto the track and saw what was left of the door handle. "Really glad we didn't go that way, right Olivia?"

Olivia gave her sister a weak smile. "Come on. Before the darn thing starts moving again."

The cousins crawled along the top of the train, not daring to stand, not daring to glance behind. The short carriage seemed as long as a football field when crawling along its roof in the dark.

Eventually Aidan stopped and peeped over the edge. "There's no ladder."

"Then we're going to have to jump," said Olivia.

Cagney gulped.

"It's better this way," said Lissy. "It'll be over quicker."

Aidan lowered himself until he hung by the edge of his fingers. The fingers let go, and the cousins heard a muffled thud.

Cagney glanced up from her position belly down on top of the train. "Aidan?"

"I'm okay. Come on, it'll be easy now."

Cagney lowered her rump, and gingerly dangled her legs off the side. Inching her way backwards she clung to the roof, a strangled cry coming from her lips.

"You've got to let go," said Lissy, gently.

Aidan offered up his arms for Cagney to fall into. "Come on sis, I've got you."

"For goodness sake, woman!" Olivia muscled her way forward and prizing up one of Cagney's fingers, levered it backwards.

"Ouch! That hurts!" yelled Cagney, moving her hands from Olivia's grasp.

"She's coming," said Olivia.

Cagney let out a squeak and plummeted over the side.

Hurriedly, Olivia then Tess turned and dropped over the edge. Lissy inched herself forward and started to turn, when the train gave an almighty lurch.

"Lissy, quick," said Aidan. "The train's about to leave."

Lissy didn't need any further encouragement. Flinging her legs over the side, she leapt, landing solidly on the ledge below just as the train pulled away and started to gather speed.

*
*
*

The cousins tore through the train. They were not sure where Pinky had gone, but they were sure they didn't want to meet him again. Finally they reached their carriage. Several colored doors stretched before them.

"Does anyone remember which compartment we were in?" asked Lissy.

Olivia shrugged. "It had an orange door."

"They all have orange doors," said Lissy.

"That's a problem," said Olivia.

Cagney quickly counted the citrus colored entryways. "Your guess is as good as ..." she finished counting, "nine."

Tess squealed, as once more the cousins were plunged into darkness. "Yikes! This is going to make it interesting."

"I'm pretty sure it's somewhere in this carriage," said Lissy. "I distinctly remember the smell of boiled cabbage."

The five sniffed the air.

"Yep," said Tess, "that's definitely cabbage."

"Then let's try this one." Aidan yanked open the nearest door and peeked inside. Even in the gloom he could see the compartment was packed with at least twenty people. "Sorry," he said, ramming it closed.

Cagney rolled her eyes. "One down, eight more to go."

"How about this one?" said Olivia.

She yanked the door open and was confronted with six men armed with flashlights, playing cards. "Sorry," she mumbled, slamming the door shut.

"In the name of Great Aunt Maud," said Cagney. "Can you guys not do anything right? Any minute now Pinky's going to find us."

Abruptly the door at the end of the carriage flew open and a flashlight beam illuminated Tess' pink poncho.

"I'm going to kill you," said a familiar voice.

Tess rushed towards the voice and flung her arms around Miss Gupta.

"For the love of cricket," said Miss Gupta, disentangling herself.

Moving forward, Miss Gupta opened the next compartment door and was instantly flattened, as five terrified children piled through it.

Miss Gupta rose from the floor and shook her head. "My father gave me one job. Look after Callie's sweet, adorable grandchildren. 'How hard could it be?' he said."

"Aah, does he really think we're adorable?" asked Tess.

"Sure," said Miss Gupta. "But let's see if he still thinks that once he actually meets you."

"Oh!" said Tess.

Miss Gupta let out a deep sigh. "We will discuss this in the morning," she said. "Right now I am going to the bathroom and would like very much for you all to be in bed by the time I return. Preferably asleep."

No one needed asking twice. Aidan and Olivia hoisted themselves into the top bunks, Lissy and Cagney piled into the middle.

"Hey guys," said Tess. "Where am I supposed to sleep?"

"On the bottom bunk," said Lissy.

"But, there's someone in it."

"Right!" said Cagney.

"No, really there is," said Tess.

"Then try the other one," said Olivia.

Tess turned and felt the bed opposite. A body shifted but did not wake.

"There's someone sleeping in that bed too," said Tess.

"Oh for goodness sake," cried Cagney. "What are you, Goldilocks?"

Olivia scooted off the top bunk and took a closer look. "She's right. There *is* someone in her bed."

"What am I going to do?" asked Tess, miserably.

"Oy, you!" Olivia poked the two inert bodies.

At once the bodies slithered off the beds. "Very sorry," they said, bowing, before silently slipping out the door.

Tess shrugged. Rummaging in her backpack, she pulled out a soft pink sarong, laid it over the crumpled bed and hopped in. It had been a long day.

24

Ishani's Surprise

Aidan was leading a pack of charging elephants over the alps. Urging his elephant on, he felt a sharp poke in the ribs and the sound of a familiar voice.

"We have fifteen minutes until the train reaches Gerta," said Miss Gupta, heading out the door. "So, wake up!"

Cagney slumped into a sitting position, her eyes firmly shut, her fingers searching for her glasses.

"What did she say?" said Tess, stretching her toes.

Olivia slid down the bunks. "She said get up."

"Yeah, that's what I was afraid she said." Tess rolled over, yanking the pink sarong higher.

Aidan yawned, pushed all thoughts of elephants out of his head, and grabbed a clean tee. "Where's Miss Gupta?"

"She told me she'd meet us on the platform," said Lissy, slipping out of the bunk and grabbing her duffle bag.

Olivia tugged the sarong off Tess. "Do you want Miss Gupta to have to come back and get you?"

Tess bolted upright so fast she banged her head on the bunk above.

Olivia dragged a hand through her scruffy dark hair. "I didn't think so."

Pulling their things together, the cousins exited the compartment and shuffled along the corridor. Within seconds the train ground to a stop and the cousins leapt off, anxiously scanning the platform for Pinky. Several people were disembarking. Luckily, none of them resembled a chubby Chinese man wearing a streak of scarlet.

Standing in a circle, Olivia was aware of someone gaining on them. A man dressed all in cream. Olivia's heart skipped a beat, but on second glance she saw this was not Pinky. Out of the morning mist, a dignified man with a kind face was approaching them.

"Greetings," he said, with a bow.

"Er, hello," said Cagney, as the man held out his hand.

"I am Kamal and you must be the Puddletons." A large smile broke onto his handsome face.

Cagney shook the older man's hand. "Pleased to meet you."

"And where is Ishani?" he asked.

"Who?" said Olivia.

"My daughter," said Kamal. "I take it she is with you?"

"Here I am, father."

Lissy glanced up and her chin dropped. Descending from the train came Miss Gupta. But Miss Gupta no longer looked like Miss Gupta. "You're … you're …" Lissy stammered.

"You're beautiful," said Tess.

Miss Gupta glared in Lissy's direction. Her long black hair was out of its normal ponytail and hung long and lustrous to her waist. But that was not what made Lissy gape in amazement. She stared because Miss Gupta no longer wore stained khaki's and an old tee, but the most beautiful sari she had ever seen. A vision in powder blue and gold, Ishani Gupta smoothly glided towards her father.

"Don't say a word," she hissed, as she passed Lissy, who stood dumbstruck.

Face to face with her father, Ishani bowed then gave him a kiss on each cheek.

"Father," she said, sweetly.

Kamal held her by the shoulders and peered deep into her eyes.

"Oh Shani," he said, "what am I going to do with you?"

The cousins followed Kamal and Miss Gupta out of the station and towards a beige jeep. Taking their bags, Kamal tossed them in the trunk while the five jostled onto the backseat.

Kamal counted their heads to make sure no one was missing and satisfied, slid behind the wheel. "Please, hold on tight. I would hate to tell Callie we lost one of you on the way."

"Excuse me, Mr. Kamal, Sir," said Lissy, "you've seen our grandma?"

Kamal turned and smiled. "She will be back soon."

Cagney peered at Kamal over the top of her glasses. "Back? But where has she gone, what is she doing?"

"Let's just say she is looking for someone. I expect her to return any day."

Olivia leaned forward. "Who's she looking for?"

"I believe your grandmother is very resourceful. She is able to find people when others cannot. A little like you, I think," he said, reaching back and ruffling the top of Olivia's short dark hair.

Kamal drove the cousins out of the small town and into the wilderness. Soon all that surrounded the jeep was dense jungle. Abruptly, the jeep took a turn onto an even smaller road.

"Where on earth do you live?" asked Tess.

"Did Ishani not tell you?"

"Tell us what?" asked Lissy.

Kamal looked at his daughter and laughed. "Then I shall let it be a pleasant surprise."

The jeep plunged deeper into the jungle. The air was moist with humidity, and the sun beat down relentlessly as the jeep slowed to maneuver around pot holes, muddy from recent rain.

"What's that?" Olivia pointed to a tower rising above the trees.

Cagney squinted into the distance at several vine covered pinnacles puncturing the pale blue sky and did a double-take. Her glasses had not been the same since landing on top of them on the train. The right arm was slightly crooked and the glass a little skew-whiff, but thank goodness she hadn't broken them. Her parents were kind, generous people, but even they had threatened bodily harm should Cagney damage her glasses one more time.

Taking them off, she gave them a quick polish before shoving them back on her nose. Glancing back towards the tower she blinked twice, just to make sure. Nope, it was official. Like a mirage, the ruins seemed to be moving in the non-existent breeze.

Kamal slowed the jeep. "It is an old Hindu temple. It has been a long time since anyone visited."

"But it's swaying," said Cagney.

Kamal laughed. "Monkeys," he said. "The temple is their home."

"Wow," said Tess, "you live in the jungle, just like Tarzan. Do you have a pet monkey as well?"

Kamal smiled. "No, little one. I have something better than a monkey."

The jeep bumped down the track, finally stopping at an ornate iron gate. Miss Gupta jumped out and unlocked a heavy padlock. Once Kamal had driven through, Miss Gupta fastened the gate behind her before slipping back into her seat.

Kamal took the key and placed it in his pajama pocket. "You can never be too careful."

The road instantly went from bad to pretty much impassable. The cousins bounced like freshly baked popcorn, as Kamal drove slowly around pot holes that rocked the jeep to its core. Finally, he pulled up in front of an elegant house with a wide verandah. Other than several jeeps lined in a row, there was not a soul to be seen.

Lissy stood and stretched her aching body.

"Please," said Kamal. "Wait here for just three minutes."

Kamal and Miss Gupta moved towards the verandah. Miss Gupta's hands were animated as she spoke, Kamal's head nodding in understanding. With a graceful leap, Miss Gupta slid into the closest jeep, cranked the engine and sped towards the trees.

Kamal returned to the cousins and angled himself behind the wheel. "Patience has never been Ishani's strong point. But then again, maybe she is simply pleased to be home."

"This is where she grew up?" asked Tess.

Kamal nodded.

"Wow, it's beautiful." Lissy gazed at the graceful house and lush vegetation.

"This is the lodge." Kamal put the jeep in gear. "But this is not where you are staying."

"It's not?" said Aidan, disappointed.

"Then where *are* we staying?" asked Tess.

"Come," said Kamal. "We go farther into the jungle."

Cagney gulped. "But won't there be tigers and things in the jungle?"

Kamal laughed. "I hope so. What kind of tiger reserve would this be, without any tigers?"

25

The Reserve

A tiger preserve?" said Cagney, gulping.

"There is nothing to be afraid of," said Kamal, kindly. "They are more afraid of you, than you of them."

"Oh, I doubt that very much," said Cagney, clambering into the front. Lissy followed close behind.

"Shouldn't we at least have a roof on this jeep? You know, in case it rains or something," said Olivia, trying and failing to sound nonchalant.

Kamal laughed. "We will not see any tigers now. The kings of the jungle are asleep in the heat. Maybe this evening we will be lucky enough to spot some."

"Lucky!" squeaked Cagney. "I don't think that's lucky. In fact I would say that would be very unlucky."

"Tigers keep away from humans. Man is the tiger's only known enemy. Why would he want to come face to face with him?"

"So, they're not dangerous?" asked Lissy, hopefully.

"No, little one, they are *very* dangerous. A single blow can kill a human, and you should never sneak up on one."

"Now why on earth would anyone want to do that?" asked Cagney.

"You'd be surprised," said Kamal. "If you are ever stranded in the jungle, be sure to make a lot of noise and they will get out of your way."

"So tigers are nice?" asked Tess.

"On the whole," said Kamal. "But sometimes tigers are bad, just like people. There was one village, not too far from here, where one tiger ate 434 people."

Cagney gulped and edged closer to Kamal.

"No one emerged from the village for five days."

"If they're going to keep out of our way, how are we ever going to see one?" asked Olivia.

"From here." Kamal pulled into a small clearing and pointed skyward.

In the depths of the jungle canopy, Olivia could just make out a wooden structure nestled amongst the trees.

"A treehouse!" squealed Tess, clapping her hands.

"I love treehouses," said Aidan. "At least I think I do. To be honest, I don't think I've ever been in one."

"But, Sir, I thought tigers could climb trees," said Lissy.

"Yes, they can," said Kamal, "but not this high."

The cousins piled out of the jeep and threw their backpacks over their shoulders.

"Place your bags inside. And take some food," said Kamal, looking at Tess. "Ishani said you would be hungry. So we have prepared."

Tess smiled. "Prepared is my favorite dish."

"I will meet you back here in thirty minutes." Kamal smiled broadly. "I have planned something very fun for us to do."

Dragging her feet, Cagney shuffled towards the rickety ladder. She would never take their spacious ranch home for granted again. In fact, if she never saw another ladder, it would still be too soon.

It took a while, but with Aidan one side and Olivia the other, Cagney was finally persuaded to climb.

"Just don't look down," said Tess, leaning precariously out the window.

Lissy grabbed her cousin by the polka-dot tee-shirt and hauled her inside. "Let's just get one thing straight. You CANNOT fly and this is not the place to test that theory."

Tess pouted. "Ah fooey!"

With much poking and prodding, Cagney finally made it into the treehouse before edging as far away from the opening as possible. "But how am I going to get down?"

"Don't worry about that," said Olivia, wiping a bead of sweat from her forehead. "I'm going to throw you."

Cagney was too tired to give any looks. She settled for a grunt.

The treehouse was airy, spacious. A plush mattress draped with mosquito nets hugged one wall and opposite sat a simple table with built-in seating all around. Brightly scattered cushions in pinks and oranges gave the treehouse a comfortable feel, and the broad open window gave a view not easily forgotten. It was just as a treehouse should be, thought Lissy. Absolutely perfect.

On the table were five knives, forks and plates, each with its own netting to keep out anything unwanted. Each plate overflowed with rice, fruit and various hard to identify food items.

Tess sighed deeply, and wedged herself onto the wooden bench. The others were not far behind.

Aidan shook out a napkin and surveyed the tiny treehouse. If only he could convince his father to build something similar in their yard, he might never have to see his sister again.

The cousins devoured the food with barely a word. They had missed breakfast and it had been a long time since they ate. For once, it wasn't only Tess who was hungry.

Twenty minutes later, the five were back on the ground, just in time to see Miss Gupta pull into the clearing. Her brow was furrowed. Her natural scowl prominent on her forehead. It was a shame, thought Lissy. If she smiled only half as much as her father, she would be stunning.

A loud trumpeting noise erupted from within the jungle.

Lissy spun around, anxiously. "What's that?"

"Our ride," said Kamal, emerging from the trees.

All of a sudden the foliage behind him began to move.

"Earthquake!" squealed Tess, a flurry of pink petticoats disappearing under the jeep.

Cagney stumbled backwards. "What's going on?"

"Don't be afraid," said Kamal. "The Maharajah won't hurt you."

Olivia squinted towards the thick jungle. "Who's The Maharajah?"

The leaves continued to sway and, high above the cousins' heads, a trunk appeared.

"*This* is The Maharajah," said Kamal.

"Wow!" Tess poked her head out from beneath the jeep. "You really *are* Tarzan."

Kamal sprung Tess to her feet. "Thank you, little one. I will take that as a compliment."

The Maharajah did, indeed, resemble something out of a Tarzan movie. The massive beast stood proudly before them, his trunk swaying gently to and fro, two small tusks glimmering in the sunshine. Tess couldn't be certain, but she was pretty sure he was smiling.

Miss Gupta strode towards the elephant. "Song soong," she commanded. The Maharajah raised his knee, forming a step. "Come, I will show you how it is done."

Miss Gupta stepped onto The Maharajah's knee and grabbed his leathery ear. The Maharajah raised his leg, and Miss Gupta rose into the air until she was able to climb the thick rope hanging down the elephant's side. In seconds, she sat on the red woven blanket which was anchored upon his wide, gray back.

"It's an elephantor," said Tess, in delight.

Miss Gupta squinted at her, confused.

Olivia rolled her eyes. "Elevator, elephantor," she explained. "I think you have to live with her to fully understand the way her mind works, or doesn't, as the case may be."

Seconds later Miss Gupta was on the ground once more.

"Are you not coming with us?" asked Lissy.

"I'm taking the jeep," said Miss Gupta, angling herself behind the wheel.

Kamal looked at the cousins. "There is nothing to be afraid of. The Maharajah is a gentleman. We have been friends for many years."

"I'm not afraid," said Aidan. "In New Delhi I rode an elephant in a wedding parade."

"Then you shall go first." Kamal guided Aidan towards The Maharajah's outstretched knee. Aidan took a deep breath, climbed aboard and reached for the elephant's ear. Once again the elephant raised his leathery leg, until Aidan was able to scamper to safety behind two flapping ears.

"Who's next?" asked Kamal.

Olivia stepped forward, eagerly. "I'll go next. Song soong," she whispered, imitating Miss Gupta's words.

As if by magic, The Maharajah raised his knee. Olivia looked at Kamal and shrugged. "Who'd have thought it," she said, climbing onto the great beast's outstretched limb.

Immediately the elephant raised his leg.

"Wait a minute, mister, I don't have your ear!" The Maharajah didn't seem to be listening and raised his leg higher into the air.

Precariously balanced on The Maharajah's knee, Olivia lunged at the rope. Scrambling up she landed belly down, bottom up.

Aidan glanced at his cousin and laughed. "Hey Olivia, I might be wrong, but I think you need to be facing the other way."

Olivia opened her eyes. Sure enough, she faced The Maharajah's tail. "Oopsies," she said, scampering around on the blanket.

"Next?" said Kamal.

"I'll go with her." Cagney motioned towards the jeep.

Miss Gupta rolled her eyes, but didn't protest.

Finally, Kamal and the others were perched on top of the gigantic beast, while Cagney and Miss Gupta sat in the jeep.

"Pai," said Kamal. The Maharajah turned his broad body and headed into the jungle.

"Yikes!" said Tess, ducking a low swinging branch, as the elephant ambled through the trees.

"How old is The Maharajah?" asked Olivia.

Kamal smiled at Olivia's interest. "The Maharajah is still very young, he is only twenty."

"How old will he get?" asked Aidan.

"Elephants can live to be as old as sixty," said Kamal. "But they rarely reach seventy. By then their teeth have started to rot, and they cannot eat enough to survive."

"Oh, that's sad." Tess slid her hand over The Maharajah's freckled rump. "I wish you could come live with me. I always get enough food, right Olivia?"

Olivia could vouch for that. But Olivia doubted even Tess could keep up with The Maharajah's eating schedule. "What does Maharajah mean?"

"I know," said Aidan. "It is Sanskrit for Great King."

"Yes," said Kamal. "Smart boy."

"Are there a lot of elephants in India?" asked Olivia.

"Yes, India has more Asian elephants than any other country, roughly between 10,000 and 15,000."

Lissy peered into the jungle as if expecting to see them all at once. "Wow! That's a lot."

"Of course, there are many more African elephants, roughly 300,000," said Kamal.

"Is there a difference between African and Indian elephants?" Olivia asked.

"Indian elephants are a lot smaller than African," explained Kamal.

"Smaller?" said Aidan. "These are *small*?"

"Compared with their African cousins they are. However, the most obvious difference is their ears. African elephants have much larger ears."

"Like Dumbo," said Lissy.

"So that's what happened," said Tess. "Dumbo was given to Indian elephants, instead of African. Who knew! Dumbo was adopted, just like me."

Kamal laughed. "You might be right, little one."

Lissy shifted her position on the blanket. It was not the most comfortable ride she had ever had. "Excuse me, Sir, but where are we going?"

"We are checking the reserve. Ishani has told me Dingbang Fat is in the vicinity. We are concerned for our tigers."

"Do you always ride on an elephant?" asked Aidan.

"Sometimes, but normally we travel by jeep. I thought this might be more fun for you."

"It's great," said Olivia, a broad smile on her face.

"Here," said Kamal, "would you like me to teach you how to steer."

Olivia's jaw fell open. "Really?"

Kamal patted The Maharajah's bristly neck. "Scoot up here next to me."

Olivia scrambled forward and Kamal showed Olivia how to nudge the elephant behind his left ear to make him turn right. She listened intently, as

Kamal taught her how to guide The Maharajah through the jungle. Swaying back and forth, Olivia thought this might well be the best day of her life.

"You are a natural, little one," said Kamal, smiling with joy.

All of a sudden The Maharajah entered a clearing and drew to a halt behind the jeep. Miss Gupta was pacing, a worried expression on her face.

"What is it, Ishani?" asked Kamal.

"Father," she said, "it is as I feared. We have poachers."

*
*   *
   *

26

Tracks

Miss Gupta pointed into the distance. "Listen."

Aidan strained his ears. He could just hear the faint noise of a car engine.

Miss Gupta slipped behind the wheel, jammed the jeep into gear and revved the engine. Glancing at Cagney she slammed her foot to the floor. "Hang on!" The jeep shot forward like a missile, Miss Gupta's headscarf flying behind like the tail of a kite.

Kamal raised his eyes. "I wanted a son," he said to Olivia.

Olivia folded her arms across her chest and took a deep breath. "Really?"

"Oh no, little one, I adore my Shani, but I don't think a boy would worry about what he wore in front of his father."

"So you know?" asked Lissy.

"Oh yes, I know. It is hard for independent women in India. Many of them live in fear of what their family expects."

"That's dreadful." Olivia had refused to wear a dress since the age of three. Right now she thanked her lucky stars she had not grown up in India and had parents who cared less about what she wore and more about grades.

Kamal nodded. "But I … I am not so old fashioned. All I expect from my daughter is for her to be happy, to be who she is."

Lissy leaned forward and whispered in Kamal's ear. "Maybe you need to tell her that."

Kamal smiled. "Callie was right about you. But clothing aside, I still think a boy could not possibly be as much trouble as Shani."

Lissy grinned.

"Hang on tight. We had better go after her. 'Pai'," Kamal commanded, and The Maharajah broke into a trot.

Riding an elephant at full speed through the jungle was a lot different than a leisurely stroll. But soon The Maharajah got into a rhythm, and the cousins rocked back and forth as he trampled his way through the greenery.

Clinging on, they tore past immense trees and a ruined temple wrapped in creepers; yet another structure reclaimed by the jungle. Several minutes later The Maharajah slowed and came to a halt by the side of the jeep containing a pale, disheveled Cagney.

"Did you see them?" asked Kamal.

Ishani turned to her father with tears in her eyes. "They've got Sashi."

Miss Gupta's pretty face was anxious and drawn. "We must find how they got in before they return. And then we must go in search."

Kamal nodded, gravely. "We will take the jeep," he said, descending gracefully from The Maharajah's back.

"And the children?" asked Miss Gupta.

"They will take The Maharajah and return to the treehouse before it gets dark."

"Who us?" squeaked Cagney.

"Come, little one." Kamal helped Cagney out of the jeep. "It is not as bad as you fear."

"I think you're seriously underestimating my fear level," muttered Cagney, dragging her feet. Shutting her eyes, Cagney felt herself tossed upwards and, within seconds, sat ten feet in the air.

Kamal looked at Olivia and smiled. "Do not be afraid, little one. The Maharajah likes you, I can tell. Besides, he could find his way through this jungle blindfolded."

"I'm not afraid," said Olivia.

Kamal nodded.

"I'm afraid," said Cagney.

"Then be brave, little one." Kamal patted The Maharajah's long trunk and said, in a commanding voice, "Treehouse."

The Maharajah turned and headed back along the trampled path. Everyone grew silent as the jeep roared in the opposite direction.

"Cagney, you've got to let go of my waist," complained Olivia. "Your camera's digging in my back."

Tess wrapped her arms around her terrified cousin and gave her a squeeze. "Don't worry. I've got you."

"You've got me, but who's got you?" asked Cagney, opening an eye.

"Olivia's got her, she's got all of us," said Aidan. "Have you ever known an animal that didn't instantly love her?"

Cagney gulped. "Do you really know how to steer this thing?"

"Yeah," said Olivia. "I really think I do."

By the time The Maharajah reached the abandoned temple, the sun was a glowing ball, perched atop the canopy. The jungle was alive with the chatter of wildlife, and the temple they had previously passed at great speed, rose towering above the cousins' heads.

Lissy gazed anxiously into the jungle. "What's that noise?"

"It doesn't sound very pleasant," said Aidan.

Olivia wrinkled her nose. "And what's that smell?"

Everyone turned towards Tess. "Hey, it's not me," said Tess, indignantly.

"It's me," said Cagney, blushing. "It's that darn food I ate on the train. I knew I should have kept to the Twinkies."

"Yikes!" Olivia wafted away the noxious fumes.

"Quick," said Cagney, "Let me off."

"What now?" said Olivia.

"Yes now," said Cagney, lunging towards the rope.

"It was the stuff in the green wrapper," said Tess. "I always make it a rule not to eat stuff in green wrappers."

Cagney's stomach let out a frightening gurgle and Olivia brought The Maharajah to an abrupt halt. Cagney slithered down his back and scurried towards the temple, her knees clenched, her scented tissues in her hand.

"Should someone go with her?" asked Lissy, reaching for the rope.

A loud noise erupted from behind the stone walls. "Be my guest," said Aidan.

Lissy let the rope go. "Maybe not."

Five minutes later, and with no Cagney in sight, the cousins slid off The Maharajah and wandered through the ruins. Now they weren't rushing past at 100 miles an hour, they could appreciate its beauty.

The temple comprised of a solid square base that tapered into delicate peaks. Although it was covered in vines, the cousins could still make out the intricate stonework amongst the decay.

They had been exploring for several minutes when Aidan gave a shout. "Guys, come look at this."

The girls darted over to where Aidan stood at the edge of the dense jungle.

"They're so pretty." Tess pulled one of the over-sized leaves towards her and draped it around her.

"Well yes, the leaves are amazing, Tess, but that wasn't what I was looking at."

"Then what *were* you looking at?" asked Olivia, pulling two tiny flashlights from her back pocket and handing one to Aidan.

"These." Aidan pointed at tire tracks leading into the jungle and lifting a giant leaf he disappeared behind it.

"Aidan, come back," said Lissy.

Aidan's voice grew muffled. "Won't be a sec."

"Great," said Lissy, looking around. "And then there were three."

Tess wandered towards a large tree on the edge of the clearing. "Wow! Something scratched the heck out of this tree."

Olivia joined her sister and rubbed her fingers along the shredded bark. "Looks like someone had a bad day."

"Who's having a bad day?" asked Lissy.

"Whoever made a mess of this tree," said Tess.

Lissy stared at her cousins, then back at the tree. "Those are tiger marks."

"Never," said Olivia, flashing the light up and down the tree. "A tiger couldn't get that high."

"Yes, they could," said Lissy, "and what's worse, they look recent – very recent."

"What's recent?" asked Aidan, reappearing.

"Aidan!" said Lissy. "You shouldn't go into the jungle alone – you could get lost."

"What, with *my* fabulous sense of direction? Anyway, what are you looking at?"

"These." Olivia pointed at the gouged tree.

"Whoa! We better get out of here before whatever made those comes back."

Olivia rolled her eyes. "As soon as your sister finishes, we will."

Lissy swept a leaf out of Aidan's wavy hair. "Did you find anything?"

"I did," said Aidan. "I found the boundary fence and what's more, I found the way the poachers got in."

"That's great," said Lissy. "We can tell Miss Gupta and Kamal when they get to the treehouse."

"Tell Miss Gupta what?" said Cagney, emerging from behind the temple.

"Tell her …"

But Aidan did not have time to finish his sentence. With an ear-splitting shriek, Cagney disappeared.

27

Disaster

A idan gazed at the spot where seconds before Cagney had stood.

"Where'd she go?" asked Lissy.

Tess shut her eyes, then opened them again. "It's magic."

"I'm down here," came a shaky voice.

Olivia sprinted to where Cagney had stood. Aiming the flashlight down, she peered into a deep hole and at a disoriented Cagney slumped at the bottom.

"It's a tiger trap," said Lissy.

"You don't say," said Cagney. "Just get me out of it."

"Can you climb?" asked Aidan.

Cagney rose to her feet and smoothed her hair in a dignified fashion. The hole was not wide, but it was deep — very deep. Placing her foot on the wall of earth she scrambled up a couple of feet before the sides gave way and she fell in an avalanche of dirt.

Lissy peered over the edge. "Are you okay?"

"Pluh!" said Cagney. "Do I look okay?"

"She's fine," said Olivia.

Cagney crouched at the bottom of the pit, felt for her glasses and promised never to be mean again.

"We're going to have to find you something to climb," said Aidan.

By now it was growing dark. The glowing amber ball was sinking fast, and long shadows reminded Aidan that night was not far behind.

Aidan and Olivia searched the perimeter of the ruins.

"What I wouldn't give for a ladder," said Olivia.

"Aha," said Tess. "All we have are those long creepy vines, right Olivia?"

Olivia eyed her sister and shook her head. "Once again, Sherlock solves the case. Come on guys, help me disentangle this vine and get it into the hole. Cagney can use it to climb."

The four cousins grabbed the heavy vine trailing around the ruin and heaved. Slowly the vine came loose enough to move.

"Watch out, Cagney, we have incoming." Aidan lowered the end of the vine into the hole.

"Excellent," said Olivia. "Our problems are solved."

"Not quite," said Tess.

Aidan smacked his head with the back of his palm and closed his eyes. "I forgot. There's no way she'll be able to climb out."

The four cousins lay on their bellies, heads hanging over the tiger trap and tried to coax Cagney up the vine.

"Lean back," said Aidan.

"Push with your toes," said Olivia.

"Pretend you have wings," said Tess.

"Wings?" said Lissy.

"It works for me," said Tess.

"It's no use," wailed Cagney, collapsing back into the pit for the fifteenth time. "I'm going to be stuck here forever."

"Come on, Cagney. I know you can do it," said Lissy, gently.

Cagney slouched in a dejected pile. The pit smelled like a Texas trash can the day before pick-up. And it was cold. Stuck in the moldy tomb, Cagney was sure things couldn't get any worse. A rustling in the corner made her realize they could. Cagney edged away from the noise and heard something hiss behind her.

"I ... can't ... do it," she sobbed.

Olivia took off her Red Sox cap and placed it on top of a pile of leaves. "Okay. Then I'm coming in and I'll push you out."

"No!" pleaded Cagney. "I don't want you to get stuck too."

Cagney's voice sounded very small. She took a deep breath and tried to sound brave, but her words came out in sobs. "And ... I think ... I think there's a snake in here."

Aidan and Olivia stared at each other. Aidan went visibly pale. Olivia shone her flashlight into the gloom and placed her hands on her hips. "Then climb," she demanded. "Or I'm coming down."

Cagney struggled to her feet, secured her camera around her neck and grabbed the vine. Placing her back against one side of the hole and her feet against the other, she tugged on the vine. Slowly, she began to rise. Inch by inch she made her way upward. Grunting with exertion, Cagney made it to within a foot of the top before she lost her footing.

As she started to tumble, Aidan lunged forward and grabbed his sister's wrist. With the added weight, his body plunged over the edge, and Aidan began to topple, head first, into the hole.

Olivia, Lissy and Tess simultaneously dived at his disappearing legs. Olivia caught his right foot and Lissy and Tess his left. Immediately the girls brought his descent to a shuddering stop.

"Guh!" said Aidan, as his body jolted, all air wrenched from his lungs.

"Pull!" screamed Olivia.

The girls staggered to their feet and started yanking. Aidan's body slowly re-emerged and hanging, like a rag doll in his arms, was Cagney's limp body.

The five collapsed in a heap, struggling to get their breath.

Cagney let out a sob. "I'm going to die."

Lissy reached for Cagney's hand. "No you're not. The worst is over."

"No it's not. I might as well die here in the jungle, because if I go home with these," Cagney removed her glasses, "my parents will kill me."

Lissy leaned forward and prized what was left of Cagney's glasses from her hands. The frames were mangled, the glass was crushed. "A bit of duct tape and some glue and they'll be … Actually, to be honest," Lissy handed the glasses back to Cagney, "you're toast."

Cagney tried to give her cousin a look, but it was kind of hard when she couldn't focus.

Suddenly, the ground began to tremble.

Lissy looked up and saw a huge shadow rushing towards them. "Watch out!" she cried, throwing her arms on top of her head.

Olivia squinted into the darkness. The Maharajah was thundering towards them.

Cagney couldn't see anything, but she could hear. "I take it all back. I don't really want to die in the jungle."

Letting out a mighty honk, The Maharajah charged to within feet of the cousins. Just when Olivia thought they would be squished like an armadillo on a Texas toll road, he veered into the jungle.

The cousins slumped on the jungle floor, a tangled, disheveled mess. Finally, Aidan hoisted himself to his knees and inspected the scrapes on his arms. "What's got into him?"

A rumbling growl pierced the air.

"Goodness, Cagney, your stomach still sounds iffy," said Lissy.

"That's not my stomach," said Cagney, wiping her eyes.

"Then who's making growling noises?" asked Olivia.

Tess pointed at two amber eyes charging out of the jungle towards them. "He is."

28

The King is Dead

Olivia wrenched Tess to her feet and dragged her towards the ruins. "Run!"

The tiger crashed out of the jungle and careened towards the temple. Hurtling in their direction, the tiger appeared larger in every bound. Backed against the ruins the cousins had nowhere else to go.

"Quick, who was the god Dinkar prayed to? The one who stops disasters?" asked Cagney.

"I think you mean the god of protection," said Lissy.

"This is no time for details," yelled Cagney. "What was his name?"

"Vishnu!" said Aidan.

Cagney sank to her knees and slapped her hands together, but it was too late, in one final bound, the tiger flew towards them. Cagney focused on his gleaming eyes, felt the rumble of his menacing growl, and glimpsed the orange flash of his tail as he fell straight down the tiger trap.

Cagney let out a strangled cry.

"I'm right with you, sister." Aidan's knees buckled as he slid down the stone ruins. The others joined them, huddled in dazed silence; a silence broken only by the thrashing of an irate tiger.

"Do you think he can get out?" asked Tess.

"Don't even go there," said Cagney.

"I'm sure he can't," said Lissy. "That trap's at least fifteen feet deep. I don't think even a tiger can jump that far."

"Even a really mad tiger?" asked Tess.

"I'm not hanging around here to find out." Cagney clambered to her feet. "I'm heading back to the treehouse."

"I'm with her, right Olivia?" said Tess.

"And how do you think you're going to get there?" asked Olivia. "Our ride deserted us, remember?"

Tess and Cagney froze.

"Have I mentioned how much I hate India?" said Cagney.

"Several times," said Olivia.

"I guess we'll have to walk," said Lissy.

"Yeah," said Tess. "Before Mr. Stripey Pants does the winning high jump in the Tiger Olympics."

Olivia looked puzzled. "You know there's something really freaky about this."

"You don't say," said Cagney.

"What's freaky?" asked Aidan. "You know, apart from the obvious."

"I'm wondering why The Maharajah charged us?"

Cagney's finger flicked towards the tiger hole. "Wow! I can't imagine."

"But elephants aren't scared of tigers," said Olivia.

"They're not?" said Tess.

"No, elephants aren't really scared of anything. They're so huge they don't have to be."

Lissy squinted towards the ruins. "Then I wonder what spooked him?"

"I still say it was Mr. Stripey Pants," said Tess. "He sure as heck scares me."

As if in confirmation, the tiger let out an almighty roar.

"That's it," said Cagney. "I'm out of here."

"Wait," said Aidan. "I hear something."

"You hear a really mad tiger," said Cagney.

"No, I hear something else." Aidan held up his hand for the girls to be quiet.

Cagney strained her ears. Apart from the grumblings of Mr. Stripey Pants, the once lively jungle was quiet as a hedgehog. At once, Cagney realized what Aidan was talking about. In the distance, the throbbing of an engine could just be heard.

"Yes! We're saved." Tess did a twirl and started her happy dance.

"About time." Cagney smoothed her frizzy curls and attempted to wipe the dirt from her ruined shorts. She quickly realized it was a lost cause.

"I hope Miss Gupta won't be too mad at us," said Lissy.

"Hey, we've found a tiger trap and discovered the way poachers get in. She'll probably be dancing the happy dance with Tess," said Olivia.

"About that hole in the fence." Aidan looked worried.

"What about it?" asked Cagney.

"I hate to burst your bubble, but I think that's the direction the sound's coming from."

"You've *got* to be joking," said Cagney.

Tess stopped in mid wiggle. "Joking about what?"

Lissy focused on the direction of the increasing engine noise. "What Aidan's saying, is that might not be Kamal's jeep."

Tess lowered her arms. "What is it then?"

Olivia nodded towards the tiger pit.

"Yikes!" said Tess.

While the cousins were rescuing Cagney, night had arrived; and, sure enough, two headlights shone through the darkness.

"Quick! Hide!" said Olivia.

The cousins tore towards the edge of the ruins and darted behind an ornately carved wall. Seconds later a truck burst into the clearing and screeched to a halt.

"My pink barrettes don't have a good feeling about this," said Tess.

The doors to the truck flung open. Olivia could see the outline of two men. Carefully they approached the tiger trap and peered down. They were greeted with a roar, making the hair on Olivia's neck stand on tip-toe.

"Boss, boss. Come quick. We have a new friend."

"You don't say," replied the boss.

Through the darkness, Olivia could just make out a third man. In one hand he held a flashlight, in the other a gun. As the beam of light darted about, Olivia caught a glimpse of a cream suit.

Tess sneezed and Lissy gasped.

"I can't believe it's really him," said Tess. "Why that evil, good for nothing…"

"Sssh," said Aidan, putting a finger under Tess' wriggling nose. "This is not a good time to be caught."

Aidan watched, frozen, as Pinky threw the flashlight to one of the poachers. As he pointed its beam into the tiger trap, Pinky aimed the gun into the pit, fired and reloaded. The single shot and Cagney's scream rang together into the night.

Pinky spun around. "What was that?"

"Nothing to worry about, boss," said the larger of the two men. "The jungle is alive at night – well, most of it is." Grabbing a ladder off the top of the truck, he tossed one end into the pit and started down the rungs.

Tess buried her face in her pink flowery hankie and started to cry. "I can't believe he did that."

The cousins were silent as they watched the poachers throw a thick net into the hole and attach a rope to the rear of the truck. The engine revved and slowly the lifeless tiger ascended from its grave.

All of a sudden the ground shook and the trees started to sway. The three men swung around, confused.

"What is it?" squeaked Pinky.

The two men looked up, eyes wide with terror.

"It is the tiger demon," one shouted.

"He is coming to eat us," shouted the other.

The smaller man unclipped the net and jumped into the truck.

"Come on!" shouted the larger man.

Pinky glowered as the smaller man roared the engine to life.

"I'm not going any–"

The large man scooped Pinky up and tossed him over his shoulder.

"Hey! Put me down!" Pinky kicked and writhed like a sack of albino pigs, but it was no good. The larger man wrenched open the truck door and hurled Pinky into the passenger seat, before diving in behind him. The truck did the fastest three point turn in the history of the universe before lurching into the jungle.

Tess' eyes were wet with tears. "Is it really the ghost of the tiger?"

"No, you big lummox. It's The Maharajah," said Olivia, as the elephant lumbered from the shadows.

"Do you think he'll charge again?" asked Cagney.

"I don't think so," said Olivia, approaching The Maharajah cautiously. "It's like he knew they were coming. Maybe that's why he took off into the jungle. It's okay, boy," she said softly, rubbing his trunk.

"Guys, come here." Aidan bent over the lifeless body of the tiger. "Look," he said, pointing at a large dart sticking out the tiger's back.

"I can't," sobbed Tess, her nose running, her eyes swollen.

Olivia drew her sister towards her. She lay Tess' sniveling head on her tummy while the Maharajah's trunk curled around the two like a fatherly embrace.

"But, Tess," said Aidan. "He's not dead."

"He's not?" said Olivia, pushing Tess and, more importantly, her nose away.

Olivia rushed over and inspected the huge cat. "He's asleep," she said, grabbing the tranquilizer Pinky had dropped.

"Thank goodness." Tess sunk to her knees and threw her arms around the giant cat.

Cagney raised her camera and snapped. "They'll never believe me back home if I don't have proof."

Aidan plucked the dart out of the tiger's side and tossed it into the hole.

"Do you think it's okay to leave him?" asked Lissy.

Cagney zoomed in on the sleeping tiger and fired off several blinding flashes. "Of course it's okay to leave him. You think we should hang around and feed him chicken soup 'til he's feeling better?"

"She's right," said Olivia. "He could wake up any time."

Lissy sighed. "But what if the poachers return and capture him before he's fully awake?"

"She has a point," said Tess.

"What if he wakes up and eats us?" asked Cagney.

"She has a better one," said Tess.

"How about we get on The Maharajah and wait," said Aidan. "I doubt he'll attack us on The Maharajah."

Each of the cousins gave the tiger a final stroke goodbye. Even asleep, the magnificent beast emanated power and beauty. Rising to their feet, the five headed towards the elephant.

Olivia tapped The Maharajah's left leg and he lifted his knee obediently. Grabbing his leathery ear, she rose into the air and scrambled onto his broad back. The others followed, leaving all but Cagney, who stood on the ground facing her fear.

A sudden roar made Cagney's heart flip. Her eyes, although fuzzy, had grown accustomed to the inky darkness, and scanning the ground Cagney realized one important thing. The tiger was no longer there.

"Cagney! Quick!" screamed Lissy.

Cagney stumbled towards The Maharajah, turning briefly to see a pair of amber eyes heading straight towards her.

29

Long Live the King

The tiger paced towards Cagney's paralyzed body. Throwing back his head he let out a chilling roar. Closer and closer his huge feet padded, until Cagney could feel his warm breath inches from her face.

Suddenly he stopped. The piercing eyes blinked, and with one last stare he turned and disappeared into the jungle. Cagney did not wait for a second chance. She hoisted herself onto The Maharajah's outstretched knee, grabbed his ear and climbed the rope.

Sitting on top of The Maharajah's broad back, Cagney shook like a maraca. Lissy put a comforting arm around her.

"He really *is* the king of the jungle," said Tess.

"You know," said Cagney, pulling herself together. "I think you're right."

The Maharajah was as good as Kamal's word, and found his way through the moonlit jungle with no problem. An hour later, Olivia spied the flickering lights of the treehouse. Never had she been so glad to see Miss Gupta.

Miss Gupta flew down the treehouse ladder. "For the love of ping-pong! Where have you been?"

The cousins tumbled off The Maharajah and began to talk at once.

"See what I have put up with?" said Miss Gupta to Kamal, who looked pale as he trotted to join them.

"Children," said Kamal, "please!"

Everyone stopped, got their breath and then the story about the poachers toppled out. Kamal's face became serious.

"There is no time to lose," he said. "Let's head to the temple and find those tracks."

"Us too?" asked Olivia, hopefully.

"Of course," said Kamal.

Everyone hurried to the jeep and squished in. Miss Gupta eyed the cousins and shook her head.

Kamal patted her hand. "I know, Ishani, but it will save time, precious time, if we don't have to drive around and search for tracks."

Ishani bowed her head. "Yes, Father."

"Can you show us exactly where you found the tracks, Aidan?" asked Kamal.

Aidan let out a long breath. "Yes, Sir. I think I can."

Miss Gupta rammed the jeep into gear. Tires spinning, the jeep plunged into the jungle with the cousins hanging on tight. After what seemed an eternity, the ruins came into view and Miss Gupta skidded to a stop.

Aidan got his bearings and pointed across the clearing. "Over there!"

Miss Gupta gunned the engine and ploughed through the jungle. Hidden behind the foliage was a tiny dirt track. The jeep bumped and twisted along until Aidan spied the fence. The metal was sliced open and peeled back. Miss Gupta rammed the jeep through the jagged hole, skidded to a stop and jumped out. Flashlight in hand, she scanned the jungle floor.

"Here, Father. They have gone this way."

"They can't have gone far," said Kamal. "I imagine they have a camp nearby. Let's hope they are still there."

"Hold this." Miss Gupta tossed the powerful torch to Lissy. "Shine it on the ground, and don't drop it."

Lissy rose to the challenge. She stood in the back of the jeep and braced her body against the roll bar. As steadily as she could, she focused the beam of light, illuminating the tracks outlined in the mud.

All of a sudden the jeep jolted into a deep rut and Lissy, catapulting head over heels, landed bottom down in the front seat. "What happened?" she asked, gasping for breath.

Miss Gupta thumped the steering wheel in despair. "We hit the road. I can't track them on a road."

"Why not?" asked Tess.

Miss Gupta flung her disheveled hair over her shoulder, her eyes blazing as she whipped around to face Tess. But then something astonishing happened. Seeing Tess' earnest face, Miss Gupta's anger disappeared. Taking Tess' hand, she gave it a squeeze and offered her a weak smile.

"Because a road doesn't leave track marks," said Miss Gupta.

Tess returned the smile. "Of course."

In the growing daylight Tess recognized the road they had journeyed along less than twelve hours before. She glanced at her battered tutu. It was too sad they had not been able to save Sashi or stop the poachers. It had all been for nothing.

Olivia pointed at the broken horizon. "There's the monkey temple."

"Really?" said Aidan. "It looks different."

Everyone gazed at the temple. There was something definitely wrong. But what?

Tess looked up and brushed away a tear. "Yeah. The monkeys are gone."

Miss Gupta dropped Tess' hand and gazed at her in disbelief. "You're brilliant!"

Miss Gupta spun the jeep left, clattered onto the road and tore in the direction of the ruins. "There's only one reason there would be no monkeys at the temple and we all know what that is."

Approaching the abandoned temple she powered off the road and ricocheted to a stop. "If I get any closer, they might hear us," said Miss Gupta, leaping from the jeep.

"Come on," said Kamal. "We travel by foot now."

The cousins trekked once more into the jungle. The looming ruins drawing closer.

"Listen," said Miss Gupta.

"I don't hear anything," whispered Lissy.

"Exactly," said Kamal. "For once the jungle is quiet. And for us, I take that as a good sign."

"The sign of the tiger, right?" said Tess.

The monkey ruins rose in front of the cousins. Through the growing dawn, they could make out the poachers' battered truck and something else.

"Crates," said Miss Gupta. "They've got Sashi and at least one other tiger in a crate."

Through the stillness, the cousins could hear raised voices. Three men stood in a clearing next to the ruins. On one side sat the truck, on the other three crates with two very unhappy occupants.

"That's Pinky," said Aidan, as a shrill voice drifted towards them. "Pinky's poachers have turned against him."

"But I was promised three," said Pinky. "If tonight you had not been such idiots we would be finished."

"You don't mess with the ghost of the king," said the taller man.

"Poppycock!" squeaked Pinky. "I tell you, there is no such thing as tiger ghosts."

"You are not from here," said the smaller man, crossing himself. "You do not know about such things."

"Stuff and nonsense," said Pinky.

"We want our money," said the taller man.

"And I want my third tiger," said Pinky. "And until then we have no deal."

"Stay here," said Miss Gupta.

"What are you going to do?" asked Tess, stifling yet another sneeze.

"I haven't quite worked that out yet, but I need to get closer."

"There are three of them," said Cagney. "I may not be the best at math, but two against three doesn't seem like good odds to me."

"Cagney is right," said Kamal.

"Here. This might even the odds a little." Olivia pulled the tranquilizer gun from her pocket.

"Where did you get this?" asked Kamal.

"Pinky dropped it by the tiger trap, so I grabbed it."

"Maybe you kids aren't so useless after all," said Miss Gupta, checking to see if it was loaded.

"Now, little ones, please stay out of sight," said Kamal. "How would I explain to your grandmother if Shani shot you with a tranquilizer gun?"

Kamal and Miss Gupta headed into the jungle and disappeared towards the other side of the temple.

Olivia started after them.

"Olivia, you can't," said Lissy. "We promised Kamal we'd stay here."

"I'm not going anywhere. I'm just getting a better view," said Olivia, shimmying up a tree.

Lissy shook her head. "You might be seen."

But Olivia didn't have time to answer. For right at that moment, Miss Gupta tripped over her sari and flew face first into the clearing.

The three men spun around in surprise.

"And what do we have here?" squeaked Pinky, peering at Miss Gupta. "Well, if it's not our pesky zoo keeper."

Miss Gupta looked up, her eyes flashing with rage, and wiped the mud from her face. Pinky and the two men began to laugh as she struggled to her feet, her beautiful sari soaked in mud, her flowing hair disheveled.

"Put up your hands," said Miss Gupta, without conviction.

"Why isn't she aiming at them?" asked Olivia.

Lissy peered out from behind the ruins. She gasped. "Because she dropped the tranquilizer."

Lissy pointed to where a glint of early morning sun reflected off something lying on the ground.

Both Pinky and Miss Gupta spotted the tranquilizer gun at the same time. It had slipped from Miss Gupta's hand as she landed on the ground, and lay several feet away at the edge of the clearing.

Their eyes met. Instantly they both dived towards it, but Miss Gupta's sari was tangled around her legs. Pinky, on the other hand, landed several feet short. Hoisting himself onto all fours he shuffled forward, as fast as his chubby knees would let him. Reaching the tranquilizer, his stubby fingers stretched towards it.

"I don't think so," said a calm voice.

Pinky stopped in mid grasp and raised his head like a dog. "Who are you?"

Kamal's voice was steely cold. "I'm the pesky zoo keeper's father."

Pinky made one last grab. But it was too late, as Kamal bent and scooped up the tranquilizer. Stepping over the little man, he tossed the gun to his daughter who caught it with ease.

"Now put your hands up," said Miss Gupta.

Two of the three men raised their arms.

"You wouldn't dare shoot me," sneered Pinky.

"I think she would," said Kamal. "In fact I'm pretty sure of it."

"I am a Chinese diplomat."

"You're going to be Chinese tiger bait in a minute," said Miss Gupta.

Pinky and the two men backed away and then, without warning, they turned and fled.

The tranquilizer went off like a starting pistol.

"They're getting away," said Tess.

"Not if I can help it," said Aidan. "Come on, they're heading straight for us."

The two poachers streaked towards the darkened ruins. The cousins kept hidden until the men drew level. Crouched in the roots of a large creeper, Lissy's leg shot out sending the smaller of the two men flying face first into the mud. The other man kept on running towards the road. Suddenly a heavy object landed belly down on top of his head.

"Kowabunga!" yelled Olivia.

"Get it off! Get it off!" he yelled, his arms flapping, his legs doing something resembling a samba, as Olivia gripped him firmly by the ears.

Cagney flew from the bushes and launched herself around his waist. Aidan was not far behind, diving for his ankles. The combined weight was too much. Overcome, the man dropped like a felled tree and toppled to one side.

"What the ..." he yelled, but the fight went out of him, as Tess catapulted from behind the ruin, landing with a dull thud on his head.

Kamal dashed across the clearing. "Children?"

"We're fine," said Lissy.

Kamal and Miss Gupta hurried over and surveyed the scene. One man lay knocked out cold, Lissy astride his back; the other lay puffing on the ground, four small children perched atop his writhing body.

Kamal smiled. "Callie would be proud of you."

"Where's Pinky?" asked Olivia.

Miss Gupta pointed towards the cages and there was Pinky. Face down. A large dart protruding from his bottom. Snoring like a hippo.

30

She's Back

Later that day, the cousins relaxed with Kamal and Miss Gupta in the boughs of the treehouse. The authorities had been called, and Pinky and his band of thugs arrested. Both Sashi and an older tiger named George had been released, and Miss Gupta assured the cousins they would be fine.

"What will happen to Pinky?" Tess asked, stuffing several grapes in her mouth.

"He will be prosecuted," said Miss Gupta. "Tiger trading is a very serious offense and one the Indian government has no tolerance for."

"Good," said Lissy, "I hope he goes to jail for a long time."

"Lissy still hasn't forgiven Pinky for messing with Aidan," said Olivia.

"I still can't believe you pushed him in the Taj Mahal reflecting pond," said Cagney.

Ishani whipped her ponytail over her shoulder. "You did what?"

Lissy looked down shyly, but obviously pleased with herself. "Aah, yes. Well, I might have forgotten to tell you about that part."

Aidan changed the subject. "What about the guy in the New Delhi market?"

Ishani grinned. "Once the police had the name of his shop it was easy. He was tracked down a couple of hours ago. The police said the store contained names of hundreds of traders. Thanks to you, the whole network has been completely stopped."

Olivia looked at Ishani's faded khaki pants and tee-shirt. "I see you and your father have talked about your clothes."

Ishani grinned. "Turns out father doesn't care what I wear," she said, smiling at Kamal. "Right, Father? Father?"

Kamal stared out the treehouse window, a serious expression on his face. All of a sudden he leapt into the air. "Yes!" he screamed, pulling out an earpiece. "320 to 312! We won!" he cried, clapping his hands with joy.

The cousins looked at each other and smiled. "Cricket!" they said, in unison.

"Tess, I see you've stopped sneezing," said Lissy.

Tess sat munching a large carrot. "Yep," she said, "I don't think it was a cold at all."

"Then what was it?" asked Cagney.

"Allergies!" said Tess. "I was allergic to Pinky!"

"India's been fascinating," said Aidan.

"Yes, I love India." Cagney broke open her last Twinkie.

Olivia frowned "Really? That's news to me."

Cagney laughed. "Let's just say I love it, except for the food!"

"I only wish Grandma could have enjoyed it with us," said Lissy.

A frown graced Kamal's handsome face. "Aah, yes, your grandmother."

Miss Gupta shot her father an urgent look. "They don't know about their–"

Kamal raised his hand. "I understand. But of course, it is up to Callie to tell you about her quest. Not us."

Tess dropped the orange she was ripping into smiles and leaned forward, listening intently. "Tell us what?"

Miss Gupta shook her head almost imperceptibly.

"I believe your grandmother will tell you when she feels the time is right," said Kamal, ruffling the top of Tess' black hair. "It is a family matter."

Cagney peered over the top of her smushed glasses. "Are you sure you couldn't tell us now, just in case she forgets?"

"She *can* be very forgetful, you know," added Aidan.

"For the love of pickles, do you children never give up?"

Kamal laughed. "It is only a shame Callie did not have the time to help us with our little tiger problem. Your grandmother is a wonderful woman to have around when you are having such problems."

"We wouldn't know," said Tess. "She's never around us."

"Ah, yes. But I believe you wouldn't have half as much fun if she was," chuckled Kamal.

The leaves on the trees started to sway. Olivia grinned, her dimple deepening on her cheek. "It's The Maharajah!"

Everyone scrambled to their feet and peered out the treehouse to see The Maharajah emerging from the jungle.

"And look who's riding him!" said Tess, as a familiar face came into view.

"Hello, little cousins," shouted Dinkar.

"But who's that behind him?" asked Aidan, squinting to make out the second person.

"It's Grandma!" said Lissy, recognizing the stout brown shoes sticking out behind Dinkar. She waved wildly out the window.

Aidan and Olivia stared at each other stunned. The Maharajah drew to a halt. Dinkar slithered down the elephant's back and, finding a ladder, laid it against the great beast.

Lissy watched Grandma's careful descent. "Do you think she knows what we've done?"

"Oh, she knows," said Kamal. "Callie and I had a long chat this morning."

"Oh great," said Cagney.

"No, no! She is very proud of you," said Kamal.

"So, she's not mad?" asked Tess.

"No. But she did ask me to tell you one thing."

"What?" asked the cousins.

"Don't tell your parents!"

Let's See What You Know

1. What is the capital of India?

2. Which country used to rule India?

3. What are the two main languages spoken in India?

4. Which mountain range sits on India's northern border?

5. Name India's film capital.

6. How many species of tigers are left in the world?

7. How many wild tigers are left in India?

8. What is Indian money called?

9. Name a popular Indian spice.

10. How many seas surround India?

11. How many countries border India?

12. What animal is sacred in India?

13. When was the Taj Mahal built?

14. Who was the Taj Mahal built for?

15. What happened to Shah Jahan after building the Taj Mahal?

Answers

1.   The capital of India is New Delhi.

2.   India was under British rule (between 1858 and 1947).

3.   Hindi and English are the two main languages spoken in India.

4.   The Himalayas sit to the north of India (and rise to 29,000 feet).

5.   India's film capital is called Bollywood (and is located in Mumbai, formerly known as Bombay).

6.   There are five subspecies of tiger. (The Bengal, Sumatran, Indochinese, Siberian and South China).

7.   As of 2011 there were roughly 1,700 wild tigers in India. (Although low, the census shows there are 295 more than the last time Indian tigers were counted, in 2006. The country is home to 40% of the world's tigers, with 23 tiger reserves in 17 states).

8.   The rupee is the currency of India.

9. Saffron is a popular Indian spice as well as curry, cardamom, ginger, cinnamon, coriander and cumin. Lots of "c" spices.

10. India is surrounded by three seas. (The Arabian Sea to the West, Bay of Bengal to the East and the Laccadive Sea to the South).

11. Six countries border India. (Bangladesh, Bhutan, Myanmar (formerly Burma), China, Nepal and Pakistan).

12. The cow is sacred in India.

13. The Taj Mahal was started in 1632 and completed around 1653. (In 1983 it became a UNESCO World Heritage Site).

14. It was built as a mausoleum for Mumtaz Mahal, (Shah Jahan's second wife who died during the birth of their 14th child).

15. After building the Taj Mahal, Shah Jahan was imprisoned by his son.

Author's Note

I hope you enjoyed Operation Tiger Paw and learning about the plight of tigers in India and around the world. Tigers are one of my favorite animals and I thoroughly enjoyed researching them.

In the book the cousins get up to all kinds of mischief, including playing with the baby tigers who are in the care of Miss Gupta.

I am sure I don't have to tell you that in real life it's best to stay as far away from tigers as humanly possible. Tigers, even in the confines of a zoo or animal reserve, are still wild animals and should be treated with respect.

As Miss Gupta mentions in the book, sadly, due to many reasons, including poaching and the destruction of the tigers' natural habitat, tigers have gone from eight subspecies of tiger in the last seventy years, to five.

To learn more about tigers and other endangered animals around the world, please go to: http://www.panthera.org/species/tiger and http://www.wcs.org/

Info Researched From

Eyewitness Books – Elephants by Ian Redmond
Photography by Dave King

National Geographic – Countries of the World by
A. Kamala Dalal

Castles Palaces and Tombs – The Taj Mahal by
Linda Tagliaferro

Insight Guides – India

Culture Shock! India – by Gitanjali Kolanad

Book Discussion Points

What do you think Sneezy is trying to hide by not giving his real name?

What do you think Grandma is doing in India?

We never get a really good description of Grandma. What do you think she looks like?

Miss Gupta tries to hide her fashion choices from her father. What do you think about dressing to please your family vs. to please yourself?

What do you think can be done to stop the killing of tigers in India?

What secret life do you think Grandma has led that she's never told the children about?

Do you think you would like to visit India? Explain your reasons, why or why not?

Which of the cousins is your favorite and why?

Acknowledgments

This book would not have been possible without the help and encouragement from the following people.

My talented critique partners, Lindsey Scheibe and Raynbow Gignilliat, without whom this book would have no descriptive passages whatsoever.

Close behind them come the members of our delicious Soup Salon, Christina Sootornvat, Cory Oakes, Lindsey Scheibe, Nikki Loftin, Samantha Clark, Shelli Cornelison and Shellie Faught plus members of the Austin SCBWI, without whose encouragement I may have given up long ago.

Thanks also goes to first readers, Nikki Loftin, Ellen Helwig, Melissa Fong, Holly Green and Tracie Hill.

Samantha Clark for the introduction of hyphens and Stephanie Hudnall for responding to all of my

300 emails, plus promising not to sell any of them to the press.

My village who keep me relatively sane: Jennifer Keaton, Erin Cowden, Rachel Luu, Ellen Helwig, Melissa Fong, Sophie and David McGough, Julie Hopkins, Stacy Johnson, Rega Paulson, Lisa Streun, Misty Blahuta, Kristi Berrier, Barb Cooper and Kitty Garza.

Deanna Roy for her knowledge and help and Erin Edwards for copy editing way beyond the call of friendship.

Varsha Bajaj, Nupur Gupta, Bethany Hegedus, Vivek Bakshi, Bill Chatterjee and Carrie Keith for bringing India alive to me.

Alex Sweeting, who did not snigger, even once, when answering my ridiculous questions on all things cricket.

Kristi Floyd, Jen Bigheart and the wonderfully supportive staff at Westbank Community Library.

My amazingly talented cover artist, Han Randhawa and his delightful wife, Gee.

Manu Verma for his help with all things web related, and his calming presence in my life.

My girls for doing dishes so mama could write and not have a complete melt down.

Mumpsy, for her encouragement and unconditional love – always.

And finally our wonderful cousins (all six of them) without whom there would be no book.

ABOUT THE AUTHOR

Photo by Dave Wilson

Sam Bond is the winner of the Writers' League of Texas Discovery Book Award in Children's/Middle Grade. Born in London and raised in Shropshire, Sam has lived all over the world. She currently lives in Austin, TX with two of the five cousins and a dog named Sausage. *Operation Tiger Paw* is the second in the Cousins In Action series.

You can find Sam online at:

www.5CousinsAdventures.com

or on Facebook at 5 Cousins Adventures

If you have enjoyed the second Cousins In Action book, please look for the cousins' next adventure set in merry old England. Mysteries abound as the cousins come face to face with Queens and castles, Lords and Ladies, ghosts and corgis.

29330456R00160

Made in the USA
Middletown, DE
15 February 2016